THEY CALLED HIM PETER

Written by
KENNETH F. NEIGHBORS

Order this book online at www.trafford.com
or email orders@trafford.com

Most Trafford titles are also available at major online book retailers.

Note for Librarians: A cataloguing record for this book is available from Library and Archives Canada at www.collectionscanada.ca/amicus/index-e.html

Printed in Victoria, BC, Canada.

ISBN:978-1-4269-1313-6 (sc)

We at Trafford believe that it is the responsibility of us all, as both individuals and corporations, to make choices that are environmentally and socially sound. You, in turn, are supporting this responsible conduct each time you purchase a Trafford book, or make use of our publishing services. To find out how you are helping, please visit www.trafford.com/responsiblepublishing.html

Our mission is to efficiently provide the world's finest, most comprehensive book publishing service, enabling every author to experience success. To find out how to publish your book, your way, and have it available worldwide, visit us online at www.trafford.com

Trafford rev: 6/26/2009

 www.trafford.com

North America & international
toll-free: 1 888 232 4444 (USA & Canada)
phone: 250 383 6864 ♦ fax: 250 383 6804 ♦ email: info@trafford.com

The United Kingdom & Europe
phone: +44 (0)1865 487 395 ♦ local rate: 0845 230 9601
facsimile: +44 (0)1865 481 507 ♦ email: info.uk@trafford.com

10 9 8 7 6 5 4 3 2 1

Introduction

This story is about a young boy that is growing up in Pacoima. His story will contain sex and violence in his life in the eighties. His name is Peter, he is 15 years old. His life will be turned upside down and life as he knows it will be different from then on. His family life is no different than yours. His father's name is Able and his mother's name is Sherry they loved him as much as they could. Peter had two siblings an older sister name Maria, and a brother name Robert. Peter was the baby of the family. Maria was the oldest and Robert was the middle child. Peter had friends like everyone else but in the year 1980. That year would mark the change in his life forever. In this story you will read how this innocent young man will have his whole life style change. You will see what Peter and his family; friends must do to survive the streets of Pacoima. Watch as this story of seduction, murder, and betrayal unfolds, which puts Peter's life in peril.

Chapter One

LOSING YOUR INNOCENCE

It happen on December 5, 1980, it started out as a normal day. Peter and his brother Robert was getting ready for school. Robert is two years older than Peter. They will be walking to school like they always do; they will leave their home at 7:00 o'clock that morning. Peter and Robert left their home and were on the way to pick up their friend Anthony. They always pick up their friends, on the way to school. Robert stated, to hurry up Anthony so we can go to pick up Carlos. On the way to Carlos's house they had to pass through Paxton Park. That was known to everyone that the logo gangs hang out there. When the boys were making their way through the park like they do every day, they noticed that some gang members were hanging around, by the handball court. One of them Robert knew in school his name was Ricky. Ricky stopped them and stated that you cannot pass through the park without paying. Robert replies by saying come on Ricky we pass through the park every day. Ricky stated again the only way you are going to pass is you will pay or go around but this is our park. Before Robert could say anything this older gang member that nobody knew stated that they could pass if they join the gang.

This person was known as Red because when he got mad his face would turn beat red. Robert replied that no one is going to join in your gang. Red stated that you and your homies will have to pay 10.00 each or the three of you will have to suck my brown dick to pass. Robert then stated to Anthony and Peter to turn around and go the other way. Red told his gang to stop them from going the other way. His gang did grab them and they took them to the bushes that are located behind the hand ball court. Red told Robert that they will join his gang or his friends will watch him fuck Robert. Robert then replies I don't think so. Red told Anthony do you want to join my gang or be fuck by one of the other members. Robert told Anthony that Red was just trying to scare them into joining their gang. Ricky then stated dude you are joking, Red looked at Ricky and punch him in the chest. Red started to shout that these motherfuckers cannot just pass through and not pay something. Robert replied if you let us go we will pay you the money tomorrow. Red looked at Robert and say if you have the money you can leave. If you don't have the money you will have to pay now. Robert stated that we don't have any money on us today but I can give you the money tomorrow. Red replies how do I know you will come this way tomorrow to pay. Robert replies that you will have to trust me that I will come back here to pay you guys. That was not good enough for Red. Red told Robert to take off your pants, Robert replies fuck you man. Ricky said to Red are you fucking gay dude because I am not watching this. Red replies to every member that he is going to fuck this kid and everyone is going to watch and then they will take turns in fucking him. Red told Robert again to take off your pants and to bend over. Robert refuse again Red then told Ricky and this other gang member name Chewy to rip off Robert's pants. Ricky and Chewy held him down and Red took off Robert's pant and then Red took off Robert's boxer. Red said look at Robert's cock you have a big cock how old are you Robert told Red that he was 17 and go and fuck yourself you fucking faggot and that Robert was going to kick his ass. Red replies you are in no condition to

told him to fuck Robert in the ass. Chewy replies I did not want to fuck him in the ass you did. Red turn and looked at Ricky you will fuck Robert in the ass. Ricky said no like Chewy did but Red said if you don't you will have to cut off his dick. Red was not playing around when he told that to Ricky. Red told chewy to stand Robert up and put Robert's head in between your legs. Red told Anthony Robert's friend to go and spread his legs. Anthony replies that I will not do that to my friend. Red replies OK we will not fuck him, but we will fuck you instead of Robert. Anthony got scare and told Red that he would help. Robert starting to yell Red kicks him in the side and tells him to shut the fuck up. Chewy picks up Robert and puts his head in-between his legs. That makes Robert to bend over and Red tells Anthony to go under Robert and spread his legs. Anthony looks at Red and states that Robert's dick will lie on my head. Red replies so what just do it ass hole. Red then tells Ricky to take off his pants, so you can start fucking this guy. Ricky started to drop his pants then he removed his boxer. Ricky replies to Red that his dick is not hard and it is not the same as when I fuck a girl in the pussy. Red tells Peter to go over there and suck Ricky cock. Peter looks at Red and Red tells Peter you suck Ricky dick until it gets hard ass hole. Peter walks towards Ricky his hand goes out to touch Ricky cock. Peter takes it and puts it in his mouth and starts to suck on it. It takes a minute or two but Ricky dick start to get hard. Red then stops Peter and tells Ricky to fuck Robert in the ass. Ricky takes his cock and Anthony is in between Robert's leg to push them apart. Ricky tries to put his dick in Robert's ass. But it won't fit because Ricky cock is so hard that it needs some lubrication so Red carries a little bottle of lotion on him. He tells Ricky to put some on and he does when Ricky tries again his dick goes in to Robert's ass. Ricky states that it feels like a pussy and that his ass is very tight he beings to fuck Robert. Ricky takes about ten minutes and he is ready to cum. Ricky tells Red and Red replies to take out your dick and cum on Anthony's face. When Ricky feels that he will cum he takes out his dick. When that happen

Ricky cum on Robert's back and on Anthony's face everyone there look and laugh at them. Once that happen every one took turn on Robert. When everyone was done fucking Robert it was about 9:00 o'clock in the morning. Every one put their clothes back on and left the three boys. Peter ran to Robert and asks if he was ok Robert replies no I'm not ok ass hole. I just was gang fuck he told Peter and Anthony. Robert was crying and when he touch his ass; there was a little blood from his ass. Anthony pick Robert up and Robert began to put his clothes back on. Robert then told Anthony and Peter to never bring this matter up again and to never tell anyone what had happen to them. Robert stated pay back is a bitch. Anthony stated how we can pay those ass holes back.

Chapter Two

SUCKING DICKS AT SCHOOL

Robert stated that he will not be going to school today. Peter then replied that if they did not go to school won't the school call home? Robert replied to Peter you did not get fuck in the ass like I did. I do not know what the fuck to do. Anthony replied I'm going home and Robert told Anthony no the fuck you're not. Robert stated what kind of friend are you Anthony? Anthony replied hey I did not what them to do to me that they were going to do to you. I had to shut the fuck up and help them fuck you because Red said he would do me man. So what do you what from me Robert, you would have done the same thing if that was me. Robert was yelling at Anthony I would have started to fight them for you. Anthony replied oh yeah how about that knife Red had. Robert stated that he would have die before they had a change to fuck you Anthony. Then Robert started to hit Anthony it was being to become a fight. Peter started to yell at them to stop and remember that he had to suck their dicks. Robert and Anthony stop and they look at Peter and said that we have to stick together on this and tell no one about what happen today. Peter stated that they should tell their uncle Pedro. Because he was like a god father in the community and no one could do anything without his ok. Pedro is a big time pimp, and a drug dealer. The other rumors are he can get you killed if he had to. Robert replied that he will take care of his own problem. Peter said he just wants to help his brother. Later that day Robert, Anthony, and Peter were walking towards home. That is when Peter's mom was driving by. She stop the car and asks that why were they not in school? Peter was scared to answer the question. Robert stated that he was ill and that he was coming home early today. His mom asks what the problem was. Robert didn't want to tell her that he was gang rape. So Robert just said that his stomach was hurting. Their mom told them to get in the car and she would drive them home and to take Anthony home as well. When they arrival at their house Robert went straight to his room.

The next day it was suppose be the same routine but how could it be. When Peter got up from bed he did the same thing as he always do? When Robert got out of bed he started to be moody and grumpy to his family. Their mother did not put up with that. Robert was complaining to her why he did not want to go to school that day. Peter's mom told Robert that he had to go to school so he can walk to school with Peter. Robert began to get in a rage over that comment. Their mom started to yell at Robert and Peter told his mom that he could walk to school by himself. Their mom would have none of that. She told Robert to get dress and go to school. Robert did get dress and Peter and he walk another way to school. So that they did not go through the park again because of what happen the day before. When they got to school they saw Carlos and he ask what happen to them yesterday. Robert replied that he was sick and that why they did not make it. Carlos said that he saw Ricky in second period and he asks about you. Robert asks what Ricky told him. Carlos replies nothing he just wanted to know why you were not in class. Peter then told the guys that he had to go to his class. Peter then left the guys and told them he would see them when they call break. When Peter was going to his math class he had to go to the restroom. When he enters the restroom by his surprise he saw Ricky there taking a piss. Ricky saw Peter and asks him if he like sucking dick now. Peter look around the restroom to see if anyone was in there before he give his answer. Ricky said that no one else was in here and that Ricky was turned on by Peter sucking his dick. Peter told Ricky that he did not like it and that he was going to get someone to fuck him up. Ricky told him not to worry about anyone else knowing what happen. Peter told Ricky that don't worry we told our uncle and that he was going to kill you guys. Ricky just laughs and told Peter to come to this restroom at break time. Because he likes how Peter sucks his dick and that he wanted Peter to do it again. Peter stated that he isn't going to do that again. Also he told Ricky that next time you make me I will bite the motherfucker off. Ricky replied that fine but I warn you if you don't come back there be got hell to pay. Ricky left the restroom to his class. Peter went on to take his piss and he was wondering want to do. When he was done he too went to his math class and thought about what Ricky said to him in the restroom. How can I get out of this mess he thought? He was not paying any attention to the teacher and the motherfucker asks Peter to solve the problem on the board. Peter thought how I can solve that math problem when I have bigger problem to solve. When the bells ring for break everyone left their class. Peter left his class and walk by the restroom and he saw Ricky standing there. He was not alone Ricky had some friends with him. When Peter walk by Ricky told him to come inside. Peter did and then Ricky told one of his friends to be a look out. Then Ricky told Peter to go into one of the stalls. Peter heart is pounding and he is beginning to get scared. Ricky told Peter in front of the other guys not to be scared because you had done this before. I told Ricky I was force to do that. Ricky stated will I guess you are going to do it again. Ricky pushes Peter into one of the stall and told the other guy to watch. Ricky unzips his pants and pulls out his dick. He then told Peter you know what to do. Peter then took a hold of his dick and he started to rub it to get it hard. Ricky was enjoying that but he reminded Peter that break would only last twenty minutes. So Ricky put his hand behind Peter head and pushing his head closer to his dick. Peter started to give Ricky a blow job. Peter knows he was doing a good job because he was hearing Ricky mooing and he was starting to move his hips forward and back. When Ricky was ready to blow his load, he held Peter head real tight. He made Peter swallow his load. Ricky then turns to his friend and told him, do you want this faggot to suck your dick. His name was Fernando and he stated sure we still have time to spare. Peter was really getting sick and tired of these guys putting their cocks in his mouth. So it was Fernando turn he took out his dick. Peter said oh hell no that cock is fucking too big for my mouth. Fernando just look at Peter and replied that his dick measured ten inches when I get a hard on. Peter begs the guy please don't make me do this. As Peter was talking to Fernando he heard Ricky laughing because he knew how big Fernando was. Peter told Ricky to shut the fuck up. Fernando just told Peter the faster you do this the faster it will be over. Peter grabs Fernando's cock and he starts by licking the head. Fernando starts to morn and he begins to like want Peter is doing to his dick. Peter then puts the dick in his mouth. Peter takes his hand and starts to stroke his dick. While his tongue is moving around Fernando head of the dick, which really gets him off. But when Fernando is really to cum, he shoots his load all over Peter's face. Fernando said that it felt really good. Soon the bell ring to go to class again. Peter was late going to his next class because he had to wash his face. When Peter saw Robert later that day he ask Peter what happen to you at break time. Peter told him want happen and Robert was very upset that Ricky and his friends made his little brother suck their dicks. Robert told Peter that bullshit and they need to pay for that.

Chapter Three

HAVING SEX IN THE BOYS LOCKER ROOM

Robert was very upset still when Peter met with him later that day. Peter and Robert had one class together it was P.E. the last class for the day. Peter was glad that school was almost over. It seems that he did not run into any of those guys again. Once this last class comes to an end he and Robert will be able to go home for the day. Well P.E. was over and the boys headed for the showers. Peter was at his locker taking off his P.E. uniform and then he was walking towards the showers. Like everyone does nobody thought any different about looking at each other. This was Peter first time looking at all the naked boys that were taking a shower. Peter thought to himself about all the naked boys and he was looking at everybody's cocks. He never realized that there were so many different colors and sizes. There were a lot of cocks walking around here. You have big ones, small ones, hairy ones, white ones, black ones, and brown ones. Peter was thinking about it so hard when he was washing his body. That when he looked down he saw that he was beginning to get hard. He looks around and nobody was paying any attention to him. Peter then turned around to see if he saw Robert. Robert was at the other end of the shower. Peter notice that Red and his other gang bangers were over there with Robert. They were touching Robert in ways that would make a girl scram. All the other boys back away from them; everyone had their mouth open in disbelief. But nobody stop them from touching Robert. Everyone was yelling at Robert of being a faggot. That made Red get bold and he told Fernando that they were going to fuck Robert, because Red stated, that this punk likes it in the ass. Robert tries to escape but Red bend him over and Fernando held Robert head down. While Red was insuring that his penis was going into Robert's anus. Fernando was making his cock goes into Robert's mouth. All the while they were making Robert morn and groans and he could not get away. Robert just gave up and started to go with the flow of things. Will someone must have told the coach, because Coach Carter came in to the locker room running. He saw what they were doing to Robert. Coach Carter started to yell and blow his whistle. He was yelling out all this profanity and that made them stopped what they were doing. Coach Carter made everyone get out of the showers and to get dress. He told another student to go and get the other coaches. Coach Carter made Robert, Red, and Fernando stay there until he got more help. Coach Carter asks what the fuck is going on in my fucking locker room. Red replied just that coach fucking. Coach Carter looked at Red and replied back to him saying all of you fucking faggots are going to be in big trouble. So when the other coaches' made their arrival they make the three of them get dress. By the time they get dress, the dean of boys Mr. Roger is in Coach Carter's office. Mr. Roger asks the boys what happen in the shower. Robert tells Mr. Roger that he was rape and he could not get away. Mr. Roger then told Coach Carter to use his phone and call the police. At that time Red is saying his side of the story. But he stated that it was not rape because you cannot rape the willing. Mr. Roger told the boys to be quite and don't say anything until I call your parents. Robert asks Mr. Roger if that was really necessary and Mr. Roger replied to Robert and told him that it was. Mr. Roger also stated that if you were force into this sex act that everyone was involved, your parents should know. Robert at that point was real scared and he thought what his dad and mom would think of him. Peter was waiting outside Coach Carter's office and when they open the door. Peter was asked by Mr. Roger what did he need. Peter replied that Robert was his brother and he wanted Robert to come home with him. Mr. Roger stated that you can come with us because your parents will be here soon. When we were all walking to the Dean's office it seem that everyone knew what had happen in the showers. When we reach the office Mr. Roger separated the three boys. Mr. Roger told Peter to sit and wait for his parents to show up. He then told Robert to come and have a seat in his office. The police came first and then came Peter's dad; he told Peter that mom could not make it. By that time Mr. Roger opens his door and replied to Peter's dad to come in. He closed the door when his dad enters the office. Peter was scared because he heard his father yelling and that he thought that his secret was going to come out. But would Robert rat him out for want Peter had done early that day. Final everyone came out of the office. Dad told me to come on and I look at Robert, he had red eyes like he was crying. At that time Peter felt really sad for Robert. Peter is thinking what dad will do and what he will do when he finds out that I suck their cocks. It was the longest trip home nobody said a word. But when we enter the house mom was there. Dad told me to go to my room and that they needed to talk to Robert alone. When Peter closed the door, he heard mom scream out loud WHAT THE FUCK. Peter knew that Robert was going to tell them about him. He heard Robert screaming and shouting that he was sorry. It seems that they were taking turns beating Robert. Peter could not take it anymore so he opens the door to his room. When Peter made it to the living room he saw Robert on the floor. Dad was yelling at him stating why, why, why are you a fucking faggot. I can't believe that my son likes getting fuck in the ass hole. Peter then starts to yell at his dad to leave Robert alone. Peter said to his parents that they force Robert in the shower. To do the things and that Robert was fighting back but they were bigger and stronger. Peter said Robert had no choice and that no one came to help him. So dad looks at Peter and asks him what did you do to help your brother? Peter replied to his dad with tears coming down his face nothing. I was there but I found myself frozen in time and I could not help my brother out. For that I'm very sorry Robert that I did not help you out. Peter's parents were shock at the way their boys have acted. Their relation was altering from then on they never treated Robert the same again. They were shamed that their boy had sex with another boy. Their dad thought that it was Robert's fault. Robert must have asked for it somehow. But Robert never told their parents about Peter. This was the beginning that would make Robert go insane. Because from then on everyone looks at Robert differently, no girls would go out with him again. Even guys look at him with disbelief or they started to smile at him. That made Robert's mind go a little bizarre.

Chapter Four

MEETING A NEW FRIEND

Well it has been a couple of weeks now, since the shower incidents that happen to Robert. The date I believe was in between Christmas and New Year. Everybody was on Christmas vacation when Peter notice that Robert was going a little crazy. When Peter confronted Robert about how he is acting towards people. Robert looked at Peter in a very bizarre way. Robert told Peter to leave him alone; I need time to work out the problems that I'm dealing with. Peter offer to help his brother deal with his problems. Robert just replied you do not know what I'm going through. You didn't get fuck in the ass in the locker room in front of everybody. Robert also told his little brother I protected you and your little secret. Robert had tears coming down his face. Peter stated to Robert if I could have change how I acting that day I would. Robert just look at Peter and he said I'm glad that this happen in my senior year in school. Peter just look at him and told him that maybe you can get some fucking help. Robert replied to Peter shut the fuck up. You didn't get fucking cocks up your ass. Now I have to go to court and face these assholes that made my life fuck up. Robert also told Peter nobody knows that they made you suck their cocks. Peter replied NO THEY ARE STILL MAKING ME SUCK THEIR FUCKING COCKS. You got out of it when they took Red to juvenile hall. Robert stated that is your problem little fucker. Why won't you tell mom or dad about it? Peter looks at Robert you must be out of your fucking mind. Tell mom or dad right then they'll treat me like they're treating you. I'll just keep sucking there dicks until, I can somehow have them stop having me do that ROBERT. Robert stated that they're never going to stop? Robert also said that he is very tired of talking about this and told Peter just to leave him alone. Peter left and he went to one of his friend's house that was down the street. The friend name was Eddie; he was an ok guy that Peter had him in his art class. When Peter saw Eddie in his backyard Eddie was talking to another person. Eddie saw Peter coming and greeted Peter and introduced the new guy to Peter. Eddie told the new guy to tell Peter what they called him. The guy just looks at Peter and smile at Peter he extended his hand. He told Peter that they called him Crazy "K". Peter looked at him and stated why. Crazy "K" replied why not? Peter didn't know what to say. Crazy "K" stated that he knew Peter and asks if the rumors were true. Peter just look at him and said what rumors. Crazy "K" replied the rumors that you suck cock and that your brother like it in the ass. It took Peter by surprise that this guy knew about Peter sucking dick. Peter knew that everyone knows about Robert but he thought that no one knew what he had done. Crazy "K" replied we're friends right so go head and tell us that the rumors are true. Peter looked at both of them, but before Peter could talk Crazy "K" cut him off. By stated that he and a couple of friends were at the park that day Red stop them from walking through the park. Peter look that someone just socks his kidneys. You know when you make that ugly face. Crazy "K" replied so don't try and lie about what happen I saw everything. Peter didn't know what to say, but he was getting mad and Crazy "K" saw that. Peter replied why didn't you help us out? Crazy "K" replied I didn't know you guys so why would I risk my neck. Peter look at Eddie, he had a surprise look on his face. Eddie then replied to Crazy "K" Peter was one of the guys that you were telling me about. Crazy "K" stated yes, but I didn't know you knew these fucking faggots. Peter replied that they were no fucking faggots. He also said that Red had a knife on him. Crazy "K" said yeah I sold that knife to Red that morning. Peter was very upset and starting to yell at Crazy "K". Peter was cussing up a storm when Crazy "K" said to him calm down. Peter just look at him and said you know that day fuck up my family life. Crazy "K" just laughs and told Peter everyone's life in this dump has a fucking crazy family life get over it. Life will get the best of you so you should not let that get you down. Peter asks Crazy "K" how old are you. Crazy "K" took out a pack of camels and lit one up. Crazy "K" then replied 15 going on 16 why do you want to know. Why do you want suck my dick too. Peter said I was force to do that I didn't want to. Crazy "K" replied why did you? If that had happen to me I would pull out my knife and stab that fucken's cock. That is why people leave me alone they don't know what the fuck I'm capable of doing. I keep these mother fuckers guessing all the time. Eddie replied that's why everybody leaves you alone. They also know that they will lose in a fight with you. Peter asks if Crazy "K" could help him in the situation he finds himself in. Crazy "K" replied, what is your situation? Peter said this guy name Ricky keeps making me suck his dick, and I'm sick of doing that. I'm not gay "K" and I want it to stop. Crazy "K" told Peter never call me just "K" again. When you address me you better use crazy and then use the letter "K". Peter replied sorry it won't happen again. Crazy "K" replied it better not happen again. Peter then said can we go back to talking about my situation. Sure Crazy "K" said, Peter then asks how I can stop him from making me suck his cock. Crazy "K" replied, that is easy just let him think that you like doing it. When he pulls out his dick, grab it and stab it in the middle of it. Pull the knife towards you and slice that motherfucken cock down the middle. But watch out that cock will be gushing out a lot of blood. Peter just look at Crazy "K" and said yeah right. That sounds great, but

I can think of a couple of problems. Crazy "K" stated, you have to intimidate him, so unless you like sucking his dick. I would do it if I had your problem. Peter said if I did that I would want to know that I wouldn't go to jail behind this. I don't what my parents to know about this either. Crazy "K" said, well then you can't do that. Why can't you kick his ass and maybe he will leave you alone. Peter stated, that Ricky would tell his parents that I suck his cock. If my parents finds out I might as well kill myself. Crazy "K" said you should get something on him. So you can black mail Ricky. Crazy "K" looked at his watch and told Eddie and Peter that he had to go. Peter asks if Crazy "K" can you help him with Ricky. Crazy "K" told, Peter that he had to think about that but he will let Peter know. Crazy "K" yelled back to Peter and told him to think about revenge.

Chapter Five

ROBERT'S DECISION

Eddie told Peter not to worry about his situation because he thinks that Crazy "K" will help him out. Peter replied that he hopes that Crazy "K" will help him. Peter stated that he had to go back home so he could help his sister move some boxes for her. So Peter left Eddie's house and he was walking towards his house. When is saw his brother going towards San Fernando Road. That seems a little weird because that way he will run into Ricky. So Peter did not know where Robert was going to do. Peter followed Robert and he may sure that Robert did not see him being followed. Once Peter saw where Robert was heading to he was puzzle by Robert decision. Peter was thinking what Robert was going to do there. Robert was heading into the lion den. Ricky and the other gang members had a hang out in the field where they had a broken down stack. Robert went right into their hang out. Peter could see the stack where he was standing. He waited there to see if they will kick him out. Peter waited a long time so he decides to take a closer view. Peter still couldn't see or hear anything. So he looked around to see if he could get closer. Peter got to the window of the stack and he hears people talking. When Peter looked in the window he saw Robert standing there talking to Ricky and three other gang members. Ricky was telling Robert how fuck up he was by having Red go to jail. Robert stated that he couldn't help that because of what he did at school. Ricky jumped out of his chair and slapped Robert on the face. Peter was ready to join the fight but Robert said that he was sorry. Ricky told Robert that he like being treated like a bitch. Also he told Robert that he like having sex with the guys. Ricky also told Robert to deny that what he was saying was not true. Robert said he couldn't deny that and it is true that he did like having sex with other guys. Peter was shocked that Robert was agreeing with Ricky. Robert said that Red got in trouble because he was so arrogant. Thinking to get my brother involved in this way. Ricky stated that Robert you should have come out of the closet. Robert stated what I can do to make this up to you guys. Ricky said to the other guys well he is asking for it, who wants to be first. One of the other guys told Ricky that he'll go first. Robert goes over to him. Robert goes to his knees and he takes his hand. Robert unzips that ugly cholo's pants and pulls out his cock. Peter can't believe what he is seeing. Robert starts to suck this cholo dick. Once Robert is done he does all of them and then they tell Robert to get undress and to lie down on the mattress. Ricky lubes his cock and he takes Robert's legs and puts them to his chest. Ricky then inserts his penis in Robert's ass. Peter can't believe that Robert is doing this and he looks like he is enjoying it. When Ricky is done with him the other guys go at it. Peter is so disgusted that he leaves and he waits for Robert to come out of the shack.

It was a couple of hours before Robert left the shack. When Robert finally left he ran into Peter. Robert asks what you are doing in this part of town Peter. Peter replied Robert I now know the truth about certain things about you Robert. I saw you leave our home and I follow you. Robert said you did what and why did you follow me anyway. Peter replied that you were acting weird and I was worried about you. But now I know the truth about you being gay. I heard everything and I saw you an action. What the fuck Robert and why didn't you tell me about it. Robert just looked at Peter and said I don't have to tell you anything. You are my little brother and I don't have to explain nothing to you. Peter said to his big brother you are an asshole and that I was going to tell you what happen today. Robert replied what you found out that you like given head to guys. Peter said hell no I was at Eddie house when I met this guy name Crazy "K" and he is thinking of helping us out. Robert stated is this guy white and he smokes? Peter said yes that is the guy do you know him? Robert replied yes I know him and he knows my situation. Peter looks confused by what Robert is saying. Robert said Peter you don't know anything about what's happen to you? Lets walk back home and I'm going tell you a story that happen to me. So they started to walk home and Robert is telling Peter what has been going on in the past year. Robert told Peter how he met Crazy "K" and that was a turning point in his young life. Robert stated that he and his sister was at this house party. There was drinking and some drugs at this party. We were talking to Crazy "K" and Maria like talking to him. When the party was over we were pretty wasted and that Maria couldn't go home like that. So Crazy "K" told us to go home with him because he has his own place. Maria said yeah right and Crazy "K" said my place is behind my grandma house. My grandma made a small room over her garage. I'm staying there so come all over. Maria said ok and told me to come on let's go over there. When we arrived Maria like it. But there was only one bed and Crazy "K" told me that the floor was his to sleep on and Maria and he was going to sleep on the bed. Will Crazy "K" take off his clothes and Maria was shocked and told Crazy "K" that she wasn't going to fuck him. Crazy "K" told Maria ok but I sleep in the nude. Crazy "K" asks Maria if she was a virgin still Maria replied yes I am. Crazy "K" replied back to her maybe by the morning you won't be a virgin anymore. Crazy "K" then told Maria if she had ever seen a naked guy before. Maria said not in person so Crazy "K" asks Maria if she wanted to touch his dick to see what it feels like. Maria said I think if I touch it I would want it. Crazy "K" went closer to her and sits next to her. They started to kiss each other and Maria went down on him. Maria was sucking Crazy "K" dick and then Crazy "K" took off her blouse. Maria he said now take off your bra and let see these big tits that you have. Remember that Maria had a lot to drink that night. So she did everything that Crazy "K" asked her to do. Maria did remove her bra and Crazy "K" started to suck her tits. While he was sucking her tits and rubbing them with his hands. She was getting very excited and she would let out morns and he took her hand. Made Maria rub his dick and she was getting more excited and the next thing he did was to remove her jeans and panties. Crazy "K" took he finger ran it in her pussy. Maria was going crazy and he asks her if she wanted to fuck? Maria said that her brother was in the room and that she didn't want Robert to watch. Crazy "K" told her that Robert won't tell and that he wouldn't watch. Crazy "K" ask Robert to go to sleep. I told him ok but I watch them anyway. I saw Crazy "K" get on top of Maria and he spread her legs. He then grabs his dick and inserted it in her pussy. When he did that her moans got louder. Robert then said that he saw his dick slowly move in and out of her pussy. Once he got going her moans were louder and louder. Maria was enjoying it and then she started to yell. Crazy "K" pulled out his cock and turned her around and started to fuck her doggy style. When he was doing that she was holding on to the head broad of the bed. Once in a while her hand would give way and her head would hit the head broad. He was fucking the shit out of her. When it was finally over she went to sleep. Crazy "K" got up and put on his robe. He saw that I was watching and he said to me did I enjoy the show. Crazy "K" told me to come outside that he needed to smoke. I got up and join him outside. While he was smoking I told him that I did enjoy him fucking my sister it made Robert very horny. Crazy "K" asks Robert what did you liked about it. Robert said to Crazy "K" that he like the size of his dick when he got excited. Crazy "K" looks at Robert and said are you a faggot. Robert replied that he wasn't for sure that he was. Robert open

Crazy "K" robe and look at his dick and then Robert touch his cock. Robert then told Crazy "K" I think I like dick more then I like pussy. Crazy "K" removed Robert's hand from his dick and asks Robert did he ever have pussy before. Robert stated no but I think I like dick more. Crazy "K" said then you are a virgin, Robert replied yes. So Crazy "K" said to Robert if you never have pussy don't you want to try it before you say you don't like it. Robert said with what girl? Crazy "K" said there one in the room right now. Robert said yeah my sister I don't think so. Crazy "K" said she wouldn't remember and she would think it was me. Robert said no thanks. Crazy "K" told Robert that he knew a guy that is gay and that he would let him do whatever Robert wanted. Crazy "K" told Robert that his name was Red and he belongs to a gay gang. Crazy "K" said to Robert do you want to meet him. Because I don't swing that way but Red does. Robert replied then at he would like to meet Red.

Robert looks at Peter and said that is how I know those guys. That is why they are mad at me. When I got involved with them they all told me to tell people that I'm gay. I told everyone to mind their own business. Red was trying to bring my homosexual out in the open.

Chaper Six

PETER TRYS TO DEAL WITH ROBERT BEING A HOMOSEXUAL

Well, the next time Peter saw Crazy "K" it was back in school. Peter saw that Crazy "K" was talking to a bunch of people. So Peter went over to Crazy "K" and was going to talk to him. Then a girl came and pushed Peter aside, and give Crazy "K" a huge slap to his face. Crazy "K" took that slap. When he recovered from it he balled up his fist and punched her right in her face. The girl falls to the ground and started to cry. Peter look at Crazy "K" and said why did you do that to her. Crazy "K" said to Peter did you see that she hit me first. Peter said yes but why did she do it to you. Well Crazy "K" said that she said that I got her pregnant. Can you believe that luck and that girl isn't even my girlfriend. Peter told Crazy "K" so you are going to be a father? Crazy "K" told Peter that he was already father to his girlfriend's child. Peter just look at him and said how old is your child? Crazy "K" replied one year old. I started having sex when I was thirteen. Crazy "K" also said that he is a very horny kid and when his dick gets hard he wants to put it in a pussy. Well Peter stated that I didn't come here to talk sex with you. My brother Robert told me how you guys met. Peter stated that Robert told him that you Crazy "K" introduce Red to him last year. Crazy "K" replied yes I did, because he was touching my dick and I don't swing like that. I told your brother that I knew a guy that is gay so what. Peter then said why you didn't mention that when I saw you at Eddie's house. Crazy "K" replied that it was my business to talk about your brother being gay. You had to find out yourself and I didn't know if you were gay. Because people think they have a problem like you in your issue about being homosexual. Crazy "K" said I don't have a problem with people being what they are as long as they know that I'm not gay. Peter you seem to have a problem that your brother is gay. Peter replied if I knew that my brother was gay I think I would be ok with that. It is the way I had to find out about it that was fuck up. I had to suck other guy dicks.

Crazy "K" said to Peter, you had to or you wanted to that is the question at hand. Peter replied I was force to do that, at that time I thought that I didn't have a choice. Crazy "K" told Peter everyone has a choice to make in what they want to do. Peter asks, what if they force you to do that? I wouldn't have done that and don't change the subject. We're talking about your brother, not me. Crazy "K" told Peter just get over that your brother is gay. Move on with your life and put this behind you. Just chalk up this experience that you know how to get a guy off. What you need to do is come with me this Friday, Peter. I'll make sure you get some pussy and maybe you'll like that more than suck some guys cock.

Peter was telling Crazy "K" can you get Robert some pussy so he can chose what he'll like more. Crazy "K" stated to Peter get over your brother he is gay. Just start worry about you and make sure you aren't gay. Peter replied oh I'm not gay and I show you that I'm not on Friday night. Crazy "K" said to Peter bring your sister. Peter stated to Crazy "K" that my sister is too old for you? Just tell her that I'll pick you guys up on Friday night. Crazy "K" told Peter that you will lose your virginity. Crazy "K" stated to Peter that I talked to Ricky and he will stop making you suck his cock. Peter was very grateful for that.

Friday night came and Peter forgot to tell Maria what Crazy "K" had told him. Peter didn't think that Maria would want to go. So he asks her before he got ready for the party. Peter said Maria, I'm going out to night with friends and they wanted to know if you wanted to go. Maria replied who are you going with what are their names. Peter told her that one of the guys name Crazy "K" and he asks if you wanted to go to a house party. Maria looks at Peter and she was taking her time to respond. So Peter said to Maria, well what he your answer and before you answer I know that you know the guy. Maria just look at him and said what time are you leaving Peter. Peter stated around eight o'clock. When eight o'clock came Maria and Peter was waiting for Crazy "K" to come and pick them up. There was a knock on the door Peter answering it and there he stood Crazy "K". Crazy "K" asks is everyone ready to party. Then let's go and have the time of our life. Peter asks Crazy "K" where the party is and he replied we are going to Sergio's house for the party. Peter said do I know him? Crazy "K" stated I don't know if you know him or not. Crazy "K" just told Peter go and have fun quit asking question. Crazy "K" looked at Maria and told her that she looks that a million dollars. Maria just said whatever. Maria asks Crazy "K" how we are going to get there. Crazy "K" said in my car and then Peter asks can you drive too. Crazy "K" said sure and that its time to go.

They all went in the car and Crazy "K" drove them about four blocks north of where they live. Maria asks if the place that they were going was on Fillmore St. he replied yes. When they got there the party was already starting. Crazy "K" stated that Sergio's parents were out of town. Crazy "K" went up the stairs and knock on the door. The door open and Crazy "K" said to Sergio we made it. When Peter got inside the house there were people drinking and Sergio gave them a bottle of beer. Peter said to Maria this is my first party that someone gave me beer. Maria told Peter to calm down and to make sure that he doesn't drink too much. Peter replied I won't. Peter saw people dancing in the living room and Crazy "K" brought over two girls their names were Rachel and Patty. Crazy "K" told Peter that one of these girls is going to fuck the shit out you. They both laugh and Peter was talking to the girls. As the night went on Peter and Rachel were getting to know one another. Rachel starts to kiss Peter and he like it. Peter was getting a little more excited and grabs her breast and Rachel told Peter that she like it. Rachel takes Peter by the hand and they go into another room. When Rachel opens the door they see Patty giving a blow job to a guy name Jose. Peter was thinking that it was his turn to received a blow job and wasn't the one that was giving it out. Rachel tells Peter to sit on the bed and she took off his shoes, then she unbuttons his pants. Rachel pulls off his pants and she noticed that his dick is already hard. Because when she removed his pants he had a boner sticking out his boxers. Peter was a little embarrassed but Rachel told him that she like it. She started to rub her hand up and down. Rachel knew that Peter was enjoying it as much as she was. Rachel asks Peter if he was a virgin Peter replied yes I am. Rachel said to him not much longer and she takes off his boxers. She spreads his legs and she gets in between them. She then puts his cock in her mouth and starts to suck his dick. As she is sucking his dick, she rubs his balls. Peter really likes it very much. When Rachel feels that Peter had enough she takes off her clothes and she sits on his lap guiding his cock into her pussy. She starts to fuck Peter and she rides him for a while. She tells Peter to get on top of her and to start fucking her really hard. Peter does that with no problem. He fucks her so hard that everyone hears them fucking. When Peter is done with Rachel, he gets dress and he leaves the room. Peter see that Crazy "K" is at the other end of the room. Peter goes over to him and Crazy "K" asks Peter did you like getting fuck by a girl. Peter replied yes it is a lot better than sucking a dick. Peter was so happy that he lost his virginity. That he almost forgotten that his sister Maria was with him. Peter then asks Crazy "K" did you know where my sister is.

Crazy "K" stated yes they are pulling a train on her in the other room. Peter look puzzled what is a train? Crazy "K" said go in that room and find out. Peter walks to the other room and when he opens the door he see Maria. She is sitting in a chair naked and there are three guys naked. One of them is fucking her and the others have hard-ons. While for their turn with Maria, Crazy "K" came over and said that Maria loves cock. Crazy "K" told Peter not to judge her and that Peter should go back and fuck Rachel again. Peter stated that I hope she is using protection. Peter went back to spend the night with Rachel.

Chapter Seven

DEALING WITH DEATH

On Saturday morning Peter felt like a new person. He felt like a man that did his business. Peter was thinking about last night and how he felt about having sex with Rachel. Well it was the morning and Sergio told everyone they had to go before his parents came home. Crazy "K" took us home and we were driving back to Peter house. He noticed that there was a police car park in front of their house. When Crazy "K" stops the car Peter and Maria ran into the house. Peter saw the cop talking to his parents. His parents are both very upset and they were crying. Maria ran to her mother and asks her what had happen and why are the police here. Their father told both of them to have a sit. Able was very upset and he had to tell his other kids what had happen to their brother Robert. Able told Maria and Peter that the police was here to inform them that they found your brother body this morning. Peter stated that he didn't know Robert was lost. Able look at Peter and told him your brother wasn't lost. Able stated that your brother Robert was found dead this morning by the police. He was killed, he was murder Able was yelling that while tears came down his cheek. Maria started to cry and Peter just look at his dad and Peter said

I don't believe that. I just saw him yesterday how did such a thing happen. Peter asks the cop how did he die and the cop stated that the information was not available at this time. Able told Peter and Maria to stay here with their mother and he had to go with the police to verify Robert's body.

When Able gets back home he told his wife that whoever did this to his boy are monsters. Sherry asks Able what did he look like, how bad was the body? Able look at his wife and said that he will never forget this day. Sherry told Able to get her son back to her. Able stated that they have to do in autopsy first. So they can punish the person that did this to our boy. Able was saying that the police are asking question around the place Robert was killed at. Peter couldn't take the death of his brother. He wanted to know why someone would kill Robert.

Peter told his family that he is going to find out what happen. Peter's father told Peter let the police handle this matter. Peter told his dad no the police won't find the killer. Peter stated that he knew Robert's friends better to ask them and not wait around for the police to ask the question. Able told Peter to give the police the information and let the police do the investigation. You are only a fifteen year old boy. What can you do that the police can't? If you run in to these guys or if it was one person they kill your brother. This is not a game this is for real Peter. Your mother and I can't and won't be able to live if anything happen to you or your sister. So we are begging you to stop talking this way and we are asking that you let the police handle this matter. Peter was very upset with his father. Able took his son Peter into his arms and hug and told him that they will find the killer and they will bring him to justice.

Peter was not satisfied with want his father was saying. But to please his parents Peter told them that he would let the police do their job. Peter stayed with his family that day but when Sunday morning came. Peter told his dad that he was going over to his uncle's house for a while. When Peter finally made it to his uncle house his aunt open the door throwing her arms around Peter crying and saying that she was very sorry to hear that her nephew was kill. Peter's aunt asks him do you know what happen. Peter replied no we don't know anything right now. The police are still investigating the crime. Peter asks if his uncle Pedro was there his aunt said he was and you can find him in the backyard. Peter heads toward the back where he meets with his uncle.

Uncle Pedro asks Peter how are you holding up Peter your father phone to tell me that you were coming over. Your father told me that you wanted to do your own investigation in Robert's death. Peter told his uncle yes and father told me to let the police do that. Uncle Pedro asks if Peter was going to be ok. Peter just looked at his uncle and Peter replied I don't know I guess so. Peter asks his uncle can you help me. Uncle Pedro said what do you mean by that. Peter said well aren't you like this big gangster and that you control all of Pacoima don't you? Uncle Pedro looked at him and said you told these lies. I work in construction Peter you know that. Peter replied yeah construction ok Uncle Pedro right construction ok.

Well Peter ask his uncle in your construction business don't you have people that can find out who killed my brother and your nephew. Uncle Pedro told Peter look losing a family member is hard. I'm going to miss Robert as well as everyone else is. But you cannot come over here and talk to me like you are doing right know. I don't know you told you these things about me, but whoever did tell you gave you wrong information. Uncle Pedro told Peter that he was sorry that Robert was dead. Uncle Pedro told Peter that maybe he should go home and lie down. Peter look in his uncle's eyes and said that he was going to find out what happen to my brother. If you don't what to help find out you don't have to but I have too. Peter left his uncle's house and headed home.

It has been a week since Robert's death and that the family had to bury their son. The funeral was going to be held on Friday afternoon. Peter overheard his father talking to his mother about how Robert died. Able told Sherry that the autopsy report stated that their son. Had been beaten to death and that he was sexually assaulted. Sherry was crying and told Able want did that mean. Able said that your son had his penis and testicles cut off and they were inserted into his mouth. Sherry became very upset about how Robert died. Peter was shock and he too was very upset about the report. Peter went to his room crying.

When it was time for the funeral Peter was still very upset and wasn't talking to anyone. When the service was over Peter told his family that he wanted to walk home. That he needed the time alone so he could digest what has happen in the past week. Eddie and Crazy "K" were there at the funeral as well and told Peter that it was a long walk back to his house. That he should go with them back to Crazy "K" place. Peter look at them and said ok that he will go back with them.

Chapter Eight

INVESTIGATION

When they left the cemetery Peter got in the back seat of Crazy "K"'s car. He did not say anything to the guys on the way back to Crazy "K" place. When they finally got there Crazy "K" told Peter that he was sorry about Robert and if he could do anything for Peter just asks. They are going up the stairs to Crazy "K" pad. Crazy "K" had a small bottle of jack denials in his cupboard and he took three glasses down. He put them on the table and poured the whiskey into the glasses. He handed a glass to Peter and told him to drink it. Crazy "K" told Peter if he wanted to talk to him and Eddie about it. Peter looked at his friends and said that there was nothing to say.

Crazy "K" said ok then let's honors Robert's life by rising their glasses to his short life. They all raise their glasses out of respect for Robert. Peter then told the guys that he heard his parents talking about the autopsy report. He said that Robert was beaten to death and that his dick and balls was cut off and was put in Robert's mouth. The guys were horrified by the news Peter was saying. Eddie told Peter did he know you would have done it? Peter replied by saying that the police was still investigating.

Crazy "K" said what they still don't know who did it. As he was passing a joint around to the guys, Peter said nothing yet. Crazy "K" said did the police talk to Ricky and did they retrace Robert's steps for that day? Peter told the guys that he didn't know what the police are doing. Peter also told the guys that he went his uncle and that he didn't what to help Peter find the murderers. Eddie told Peter maybe the police will find whoever was responsible for Robert's death. Peter stated, well when will the police finds out the year 2030? It will be too late by then. The bottle of whiskey was almost empty when Crazy "K" told Peter that he'll help find out who kill his brother? Peter asks Crazy "K" how you will find out that. Crazy "K" said, well start by asking Ricky where he was when Robert die. We will do our own investigation, but don't tell anyone that we are doing that. So when you find out whom did it you can do them like they did to Robert. Peter looks at his friends and told them that he really appreciates them for being there for him. Eddie stated that we should let the police handle this and to wait to see what they do. Eddie also said that the whiskey was getting to their heads. Crazy "K" told Eddie that the whiskey was getting to him and that it wasn't getting to Peter and him. He also stated that their minds were clear on what to do. Crazy "K" told Peter and Eddie that they will start tomorrow and their first person to talk to was going to be Ricky. Peter asks if he could spend the night at Crazy "K" pad. Crazy "K" told Peter sure and told Eddie to stay the night as well. Peter told Crazy "K" if he had a phone so he could call his parents that he was going to stay the night. Crazy "K" replied that he had to use his grandma's phone because he did not have one. When Peter was done calling his parents, he went back to Crazy "K" pad. When Peter was going to open the door, he heard Eddie complaining to Crazy "K". Eddie was telling him why you are making Peter think that you and he are going to solve his brother murder. Let's come back to reality we are a bunch of kids that don't know what we are going to do. Crazy "K" told Eddie that we can is catch this person if we put our heads together. Eddie told Crazy "K" we are going way over our heads on this one. Crazy "K" told Eddie we can solve this one we just have to ask Ricky where Robert went. Peter needs closure on this. Why can we help him Eddie? I'm just wanted to help Peter get over his brother's death. Peter came into the house and stated that if Eddie didn't want to help that it's ok. Eddie said fine I'll help you but I just don't want to get in any trouble.

In the morning they got out of bed and had some breakfast and Crazy "K" was in the shower. Eddie asks Peter are you sure you really want Crazy "K" help. Peter look at Eddie and said yes I'm grateful that he wants to help me. Eddie stated OK, because once Crazy "K" starts something he won't stop until he thinks he done. Eddie also said that he didn't get that nickname for being nice. That's why they call him crazy, just remember that Peter? Crazy "K" got out of the shower and came in the room naked. Peter said why you didn't wrap a towel around your waist. Crazy "K" replied why, it's not like you never saw me naked before or does it turn you on. Peter replied, no but I thought that you would come out dress. Crazy "K" said I'm getting dress now.

Once everyone was ready they got into Crazy "K"'s car and they headed to Ricky's house. When they got there Ricky opens the door. He was surprise to see them at his house. Ricky said what you'll guys doing at my house. Crazy "K" said we need to talk, Ricky replied what about? Peter said about my brother? Ricky said to Peter that he heard what happen and that he was sorry to hear that Robert was dead. Crazy "K" told Ricky, come outside and talk to us or I'll tell your family that you are gay. Ricky said shut the fuck up and Ricky closed the door behind him. Crazy "K" told Ricky let's go for a ride. Ricky got in the back seat with Peter. Crazy "K" drove them to gravity hill and he pulled the car over. Crazy "K" told Ricky that Peter wanted to know what happen to his brother. Ricky told them that he didn't know. Eddie asks if Robert was with him the night he was killed. Ricky said Robert went home and that is the last time he saw him. Peter said so he was all right so why did he go home. When he told me that he was going to spend the night with you, why would he leave to go home? Ricky replied that Robert wasn't feeling ok so he decided to go to his house. Crazy "K" just look at Ricky and said to him did you kill Robert? Ricky replied no I didn't; Crazy "K" asks if he knew who did? Ricky replied no. Crazy "K" told Peter to get out of the car. Peter did and Crazy "K" got in the back seat with Ricky. Crazy "K" told Ricky to take out his dick? Peter thought how bizarre was that and Ricky replied, why you want to give me a blow job Crazy "K"? Crazy "K" asks again to Ricky take out your fucking dick. Ricky pulls out his dick for Crazy "K". Crazy "K" takes a hold of Ricky cock and he pulls a knife out of his pocket. Crazy "K" takes the knife and it looks like he is going to cut off Ricky's dick. Ricky asks Crazy "K" want are you doing Man. Crazy "K" said I think that you are lying to us and you better start telling us what happen or I'm going to cut off your dick. Like they did to Robert, Ricky's eyes were big and he said that he didn't know who kill Robert. Crazy "K" said to Ricky, you're going to tell us who did it or I'll cut off your cock? Ricky told Crazy "K" that he did have the balls to do it. Crazy "K" told Ricky to look down and when Ricky look down he saw a little bit of blood. Ricky was started to cry and was yelling I don't know. Eddie said come on Crazy "K" he doesn't know what happen to Robert. Crazy "K" ask Peter what do you want to do? I can cut off his dick or do you believe that Ricky is telling the truth. Peter replied I think he knows something about Robert dyeing. Peter looks at Crazy "K" and told him to cut off his dick. Ricky then said that this guy came to him and he was piss off that Red was in jail. He didn't like Red being in jail. Crazy "K" told Ricky come on keep talking and maybe I won't cut you. Ricky said please don't cut off my dick please Crazy "K". Crazy "K" then told Ricky that he tells everything that he won't cut off his dick. Ricky said that Robert was killed because he putted Red in jail. It was his older brother name Pablo that killed Robert and not me. Crazy "K" then pulls on his dick and with one tug of the knife he cut off Ricky's cock. Blood was everywhere and Ricky cried out oh god. Ricky tried to stop the blood, but he couldn't Ricky look at Crazy"K". He told him to fuck off and Crazy "K" cut Ricky's throat. Ricky died instantly and that freaked Eddie out. Eddie stated that want Crazy "K" did was unnecessary and Crazy "K" then open the door and push Ricky out of the car.

Crazy "K" told everybody to shut the fuck up. Peter said to Crazy "K" you didn't have to kill Ricky, he told us who did. Crazy "K" stated that yes Ricky did tell us who did. But when we drop him off he would have told Pablo. Peter got back in the car and they drove away. Eddie said I can't believe you did that Crazy "K". Crazy "K" told Eddie to calm down and any way he deserves it. Because he may Peter sucks his dick. Crazy "K" told Peter to hold out his hand. Peter held out his hand and Crazy "K" puts Ricky's dick into Peter's hand. Peter throw away Ricky's dick out the window.

Eddie said we are going to jail and when his parents know that he was with us. Crazy "K" told Eddie that no one was going to jail and no one saw that we pick up Ricky. It was in the mid morning, said Eddie. Eddie also told Crazy "K" you have all of Ricky's blood in your car and on you. Crazy "K" told Eddie that I will take the water hose and wash the inside of the car. Eddie told Crazy "K" that the nickname fits and that he was really crazy. Crazy "K" told Eddie thanks a lot that really means a lot to me. Eddie told Crazy "K" to take him home that he feels really sick. When Crazy "K" was going to drop off Eddie and he told Eddie to stay calm. Crazy "K" also told Eddie not to talk to anyone about what happen today. Eddie said don't worry I won't. Crazy "K" said it would be ashamed if I have to do that to one of my real good friends. Eddie just looks at him and told Peter that he'll see him later. Crazy "K" told Peter to come and sit in the front seat. He told Peter that they have to think of a plan to take out Pablo. Because when he heard what happen he will be looking for you Peter. Crazy "K" told Peter to help him wash his car out. Peter said that he would help. They drive to the nearest car wash and they use the hose to wash away Rick's blood.

Chapter Nine

PARTY AFTER THE KILLING

When Peter and Crazy "K" goes back to his pad. Peter is sure how he feels about what happen earlier that day. Crazy "K" told Peter that if you have any blood on yourself or on your shoes to take them off before you come in. Peter looked at himself and told Crazy "K" that he did not have any blood on him. Crazy "K" replied well then go in the house and brings me a trash bag. Peter enters the house and he brings Crazy "K" a trash bag. Crazy "K" starts to take off his cloths and puts them in the trash bag. Then he tells Peter don't touch the bag. Crazy "K" then jumps in the shower and washes the blood from his body. When he gets out of the shower he gives Peter a number to call and he tells Peter to tell them that he wants them to come over tonight. Peter asks Crazy "K" where you wanted me to call from. Crazy "K" said to Peter my grandma's phone remember. Peter goes to his grandma's house to use the phone. When Peter is done with the phone he heads back to Crazy "K" pad. Peter then sees Crazy "K" at the BBQ and he was burning something. Peter goes over there to see what it was. Crazy "K" told Peter that he was burning the evidence. Crazy "K" asks Peter if he made that call. Peter stated that he did and that it was a girl on the other end. Crazy "K" told Peter of course it was. I want to party tonight and that I wanted someone to fuck. Or did you think that I was going to fuck you Peter? Peter replied no, but do I get someone to fuck as well. Crazy "K" said I don't know, can you Peter? Well is she bringing another girl over, said Peter? Crazy "K" said to Peter that he is very horny and that he needed this person to fuck. I don't know if she is bringing anyone else over or not. If she doesn't bring anyone else I'll let you watch me ok Peter. Peter said to Crazy "K" well I can go home and let you be with her ok. Crazy "K" said no, I need you here so we can plan are next move.

They went up to Crazy "K" pad and they waited until the girl came that Peter called for Crazy "K". When the girl came to the pad, Crazy "K" introduces her to Peter. Crazy "K" told Peter that her name was Cindy. Crazy "K" made us dinner and she brought over a big bottle of (JD) whiskey. Everyone was eating, drinking, and smoking pot. We were getting fuck up and then Peter notice that Crazy "K" and Cindy are heading to the bed. Peter was drunk from drinking too much whiskey. Peter saw them making out and that they were taking off their clothes. Peter got up from the table and he try to make it to the chair. Peter fall right on Crazy "K" when he was trying to put his cock in Cindy. Crazy "K" just pushes Peter to the chair and then he went back to Cindy and fucks the shit right out of her. Peter was watching Crazy "K" fuck Cindy. That made Peter so horny that Peter began to pull out his dick and starts to jack off. The more that he saw Crazy "K" fucking Cindy the more he strokes his dick. Peter was thinking how crazy is this he is starting to jacking off. To someone that was having sex in front of him. Crazy "K" was fucking Cindy so hard that he was making her have multi-orgasms. When Peter was hearing that he was stroking his dick harder and harder. Peter was thinking that he had never felt his dick this hard before. Cindy was yelling louder and louder the more Cindy was yelling the more she yelled. That made Peter more erratic with him stroking his dick. When Peter heard that Crazy "K" and Cindy were about to cum. Peter was there himself and the three of them all cum together. When Crazy "K" got off Cindy, he looked at Peter and saw that he was in the nude. Crazy "K" also saw that Peter also got off. He offers him a cigarette. They all were smoking and then Cindy told Crazy "K" that was the best fuck she had ever had. Peter was thinking how crazy this is, we are all naked and smoking cigarettes. Crazy "K" told Peter that we better go to sleep about. Peter woke up in the morning only because he heard. Crazy "K" fuckin Cindy again, Peter then gets up and he saw again Crazy "K" dick going in and out of Cindy pussy. Peter went to the bathroom to take a leak. When Peter was trying to go to the bathroom, is hearing Cindy screaming again and that made Peter very horny. Peter started stroking his dick again. He then began to imagine that he was making Cindy scream. When Peter was done he jumps into the shower. Peter was washing his body and when he was washing his hair. Peter notice that Cindy was behind him and she asks him to pass the soap. Peter was watching her wash her perfect body. Then Crazy "K" jump in to the shower as well. Crazy "K" told Peter if he could pass him the shampoo Peter did. Peter was shocked that Crazy "K" was in the shower with them. When everyone was done taking a shower we all got out. Cindy told Crazy "K" she had fun but it was time for her to go. She kisses Crazy "K" and said good-bye to Peter.

When Cindy left Crazy "K" told Peter let's get down to business. He told Peter how he felted when I killed Ricky. Peter replied that he felt nothing and that he was fine by what he did. Crazy "K" told Peter there is going to be more killings when we are done. Peter stated, what about Eddie is also saw what had happen. Crazy "K" said don't worry about him; I'll take care of Eddie. Crazy "K" said now let's think about how we can take down Pablo. Crazy "K" told Peter that he can't brag about what he saw and that if the police come around you just say I don't know about that Peter replied ok. Will Pablo is going to be harder because he is much older but I think we can do it. We just have to think about what he likes to do and make sure he comes to us.

Then Peter you can kill Pablo and revenge your brother death. So let see where Pablo hangs out is. Let's go and talk to this guy name Juan. Peter asks if Juan will tell them what Pablo likes to do. Crazy "K" said I hope but you never know what he will say.

They got into Crazy "K"'s car and they went to find Juan. Crazy "K" told Peter that Juan usually hangs out at the corner of Paxton and San Fernando Road. So that is where they began to look for Juan. Crazy "K" told Peter that Juan is a crack head and that he knew where everybody hangs out. Because he lived on the streets for ever that is when they saw Juan. He was begging people for money. They parked the car and walk over to Juan. Crazy "K" asks Juan if he knew where Pablo hangs out. Juan said how much is that information is worth to you. Crazy "K" stated that he needs fifty dollars and that he could tell them what they wanted to known. Crazy "K" asks Peter how much money do you have? Peter told Crazy "K" nothing and he had no money either. Crazy "K" told Juan to come and we'll make the transaction behind the building. Everyone walk over to the spot and Peter was looking at Crazy "K", because he knew that there was no money to give to Juan. When they went behind the building Juan say give me the money? Crazy "K" kicks Juan right in the nuts. Juan went down and Crazy "K" started to kick and punch Juan. Crazy "K" told Juan while he was hitting him to talk. Juan stated to stop hitting him and he'll tell you want he knows. So Crazy "K" stop and Juan told us that Pablo always hangs out by Chew's bar, Crazy "K" said thanks Juan.

Crazy "K" told Peter that is how you treat somebody that has information that you want. We have to act crazy sometimes; don't let people think that you're a bitch. Peter said ok. So Crazy "K" told Peter that we have to stake out the bar and see if Pablo comes out drunk. So tonight we'll start Peter then replied I can't do it tonight because there is school tomorrow. Crazy "K" look at Peter and told him that are you stupid? Peter replied I have to go home my parents going to want me home tonight. Crazy "K" said fine

I have to do it myself. Peter said to Crazy "K" that he was sorry. Crazy "K" stated that he'll drop Peter off at his house.

Later that night Crazy "K" stake out the bar that Pablo always went to. Crazy "K" saw Pablo enter the bar from the alley entrance. Pablo came out of the bar and he was fuck up he was really drunk. Crazy "K" also saw that Pablo came out by himself. Crazy "K" was thinking that this was perfect to grab him. Crazy "K" stake out the bar the entire week, on Friday morning he told Peter that they can grab Pablo tonight. Peter agrees to come over to Crazy "K" pad when they left school.

Chapter Ten

THE TORTURE AND KILLING OF PABLO

When Crazy "K" and Peter, was leaving their last class for the day they ran into Eddie. Peter said how are you doing Eddie. Eddie replied fine and that he stated that I see that you guys are still around each other. Crazy "K" said to Eddie what is wrong with you man? Eddie looks at them and said you guys don't any have any remorse on what happen to Ricky? Peter then said to Eddie, listen Ricky had it coming and he didn't make you suck his dick. Like he made me do and any way he help get my brother killed. So you can ask if I have any remorse for him. Did Ricky have any remorse for what he did; I can honestly say he did not. So how can I have remorse for him? Honestly Eddie you are making too much out of this. Eddie replied Peter how can you say that a person had been murder. You didn't like when you heard that your brother was killed. What about Ricky's family? Crazy "K" then replied come on Eddie why don't you hang out with us tonight. Eddie replied that I don't think so but thanks for the invite. So then Crazy "K" asks Eddie is you thinking of ratting on us

Eddie. Because you know what happens to rats' right. Eddie then replied are you guys threatening me. Crazy "K" told Eddie, no of course not I just want to remind you that you were there and you didn't stop anyone from hurting Ricky. So you are just as much in on it, as we are. Eddie then said don't worry I'm not going to talk to anyone about what happen to Ricky. Crazy "K" then said to Eddie to come on and spend the night with us. We can use your help tonight. Eddie asks what they have planned on doing tonight. Crazy "K" told Peter does you what to tell him or should I do it. Peter told Crazy "K" that he could tell Eddie what they are doing. Crazy "K" said to Eddie well I tell your plans in the car on the way to my house. So they all went and get into Crazy "K"'s car. Once they started to drive away from school. Eddie asks ok guys want are your plans tonight. Crazy "K" said if I tell you? You can't repeat it to anyone ok Eddie. Eddie thought about what Crazy "K" said and he deicide that he wouldn't tell anyone. So Crazy "K" tells Eddie what they had planned to do about Pablo. Eddie looks at the guys and stated that they are truly gone insane and that he would recommend that they both go to the doctor's for therapy. Peter and Crazy "K" laugh at what Eddie told them. Peter got mad and stated, I don't care Eddie, I have to avenge my brother death. Peter asks Eddie are you going to help us or not. Eddie replied I have to think about that for a while. Crazy "K" told Eddie come on help Peter seek justice. Eddie just looks at Crazy "K" and he said I guess so.

When Crazy "K" pulls into the parking spot they all got out of the car. When they enter Crazy "K"'s pad, he took out a duffle bag from the closet. Peter asks what that is for Crazy "K". Crazy "K" stated that these are the tools that we will need for the job. Peter asks if he could take a look inside of the bag. Crazy "K" told Peter go head and look inside. Peter opens the bag and pulls out the contents; Peter puts the stuff on the bed. The bag had a hammer, an 18" knife, a small axe, a big axe that the handle was sawed in half, duck tape, and machete. Crazy "K" told Peter to put everything back in the bag. Crazy "K" told Eddie to take the tape player with him when it was time to leave. Crazy "K" said to everybody will go around 10:00 o'clock.

When it was getting closure to the time that they were going. Crazy "K" told them what they were going to do. He told the guys that he will stay behind the wheel of the car since he was the only driver. He told Peter to take the hammer and hit it over Pablo head. When Pablo is knock out Eddie will help Peter carry Pablo to his car and that is when the fun starts. Crazy "K" ask the guys do you understand? Peter asks, do we bring him back here? Crazy "K" said no, I have a place where we are going to do this. It is an empty warehouse and that nobody goes there. At this place there is a basement, which is where we are going to revenge Robert's death. Crazy "K" told the guys it is time to go.

Crazy "K" drove to the bar where he stake out for the week. He parks his car in the alley and across from where you can see the back entrance. Eddie said how we know Pablo is in there. Crazy "K" stated that there is his car park. So now we wait until he comes out. Crazy "K" pulls out a pack of cigarettes and he takes one out to smoke. He offer one to the guys and Peter was the only one take one.

Well it was around one in morning when Pablo came out of the bar. Pablo was drunk and he told Peter that it will be easy just hit the guy. They look around to see if anyone was around. They saw nobody so Crazy "K" told Peter go and get this fucker. Peter gets out of the car and he walks towards Pablo. Pablo is so drunk that he doesn't even see Peter until Peter gets right on him. Pablo looks at Peter and said to Peter what the fuck is you looking at asshole. Peter then rising his hand and down came the hammer that Peter had. It hit Pablo on the head and he fall down. Eddie ran to help Peter carry Pablo. Crazy "K" drove his car to them and they throw Pablo in the back seat with Peter. Crazy "K" told them that he had to drive a normal matter. Crazy "K" told them to watch out for police cars. When they arrived at the abandoned warehouse, they all got out of the car. Eddie and Peter carried Pablo inside. Crazy "K" took his bag out of the trunk and went into the warehouse. They took Pablo down into the basement. Crazy "K" told them to put Pablo on the steel table. When they put Pablo down on the table, Crazy "K" pulls out some rope and tie down his hands and feet to the legs of the table. Crazy "K" told the guys to relax and get some rest because Pablo isn't going anywhere.

After a while Pablo begins to wake up. Pablo knows that something is wrong because he can't move his hands or feet. Pablo said what the fuck is going on here. Crazy "K" goes to Pablo and say yeah asshole do you remember a guy called Robert. Pablo replies what the fuck get me off this table and I won't kick your ass. Crazy "K" said that Pablo is really scaring me. Crazy "K" slapped Pablo in the face, Crazy "K" told Pablo to answer the question. Peter asks Pablo do you remember Robert. Pablo replied who is Robert I do not know a Robert. Peter said of course you know Robert because you kill him. Do you remember him now? Pablo stops to think about what Peter said to him. Pablo said I'm not going to tell you anything. Crazy "K" told Pablo that's ok. Crazy "K" took out the tape player and put in a song. The song was "shambala". Crazy "K" then took out his 18" knife and told Pablo that he is going to talk. Crazy "K" takes the knife and puts it inside of Pablo's shirt. He then pulls the knife upwards and the knife cut through his shirt. He then did the same thing to his pants. Before you knew it Pablo was naked on the table. Pablo cry out you fucking freaks what are you guys going to do. Peter told Pablo that he killed his brother and that they were going to have their revenge. Pablo was now very worried. Pablo told them that he didn't kill anyone and that he was innocent. Peter stated that you kill my brother because of Red. Pablo knew that someone told them that information. So Pablo told them ok I knew that your brother was dead. But I didn't do it, but I know who did. Peter told Pablo who did if you didn't do it. Pablo stated that it was a guy name Ricky. The guys laugh and told him that Ricky was the one that said you did it. Pablo said that Ricky was lying and that he was innocent. Crazy "K" told Peter it doesn't matter because we already kill Ricky. Pablo started to cry and said that he will be revenge by his brother. Crazy "K" told Pablo that he'll kill his brother Red when he comes out of jail. But right now we are going to fuck you up. Crazy "K" told Peter to cut him and he gives the knife to Peter. Peter looks at Pablo and Pablo tells Peter you don't have to do man. Peter thinks about Robert not having a choice and Peter then stab Pablo in the side. Pablo screams and Crazy "K" gets excited and tells Peter to cut off a ball. But don't kill him yet because I want to do some damage to this punk. Peter looks at Pablo's dick and he moves his dick to the side. Peter jabs the knife in Pablo's right nut. Pablo begins to scram and Crazy "K" told him go head nobody can hear you. Next thing Peter takes the knife and cuts off his other nut. Pablo begins to bleed all over the table. Crazy "K" takes out the machete and slams the machete into Pablo's shoulder and cuts off his left arm. Eddie starts to freak out and Crazy "K" tells him to shut the fuck up. Crazy "K" then gives the machete to Peter and he tells Peter to cut off his right leg. Peter looks at Pablo's right leg. He lifts up the machete and he slams it into Pablo's leg. The machete gets struck into his leg. Crazy "K" told Peter to pull the machete towards him. When Peter did that the machete open up Pablo leg, blood was flowing out of his body. Pablo fainted due to losing a lot of blood. Crazy "K" took a hold of Pablo's dick and cut that off and put it in his mouth. Crazy "K" told the guys to put the tools back in the bag and let's get out of here.

Chapter Eleven

EDDIE'S DILEMMA

When they were going to the car, Crazy "K" told them to stop. Crazy "K" told Peter that he had blood all over him. Peter replied so you have blood all over you as well. Crazy "K" stated that he knew that and that he brought everyone a change of clothes. Crazy "K" told everyone to change their clothes and put the blooded clothes in the bag. Peter and Crazy "K" took off their clothes and they change into the new clothes that he brought. Peter told Eddie isn't you changing. Crazy "K" told Peter that Eddie didn't have to change because his clothes did have any blood on it. Because Eddie choice not to take part in the fun. Eddie stated that he couldn't do any harm to that guy. Crazy "K" took the bag of clothes and he added gas on the bag. He lit a cigarette first and throws the match on the bag. When the match it the bag, the bag was engulf in flames spurting black thick smoke. Eddie said someone will see the smoke and call the fire department. Crazy "K" told them let's go before someone see us. Crazy "K" told them that it is early morning and I didn't see anyone around. They all got back into the car and they headed for Crazy "K" pad. When they arrived Crazy "K" told them that he was going to take a shower and that he told Peter don't lay down anywhere. When I'm done Peter you can take a shower. Then Crazy "K" told Eddie don't leave, we have to talk about what we are going to say. If anybody asks what we did last night Crazy "K" goes into the shower. When Crazy "K" is taking his shower, Eddie tells Peter that they are making a big mistake. Peter said what you are talking about Eddie. I witness two fucking murders man? How are we going to get out of this, the police is investigating Ricky murder. When they find out about Pablo murder, the police will link the murders to your brother's death. They will be knocking on your door and going to be asking a lot of question. Peter replied told Eddie that the police won't find out that we know any of those guys. Eddie just looks at Peter and tells him the police are not stupid. Please Peter don't think that they are stupid, because that will be are down fall.

Crazy "K" tells Peter to take his shower and to hurry up. He looked at Eddie and said what were you guys were talking about. Eddie replied nothing man. Eddie told Crazy "K" isn't you going to get dress. Crazy "K" said why, don't you like looking at my naked body Eddie? Eddie replied hey man I'm not gay. Then Crazy "K" said to Eddie stop looking at my DICK if you'll not gay.

Crazy "K" and Eddie just look at each other, until Peter comes out of the shower to join in on the conversation. Peter enters the room and saw that Crazy "K" was naked on the bed. Peter asks Crazy "K" if he was going to get dress. Crazy "K" told both of them don't worry about me being naked. I'm much tried and that we all need to get some sleep. You guys know that I sleep in the nude. So Crazy "K" told Peter and Eddie that if anybody asks what we were doing last night, we were parting and talking about girls. He then told Peter, the police will most likely come and talk to you. You just say that you spend the night with us. Then the police will verify your story. Eddie you have to be strong and not break under the pressure. Eddie replied how come you are telling me that I'll break under pressure. Crazy "K" looks at Eddie and said that he didn't do much to kill Pablo. That Peter and I are in much deeper trouble then you would be in Eddie. We did the killing and you just watch like a little bitch. But don't worry Peter, Eddie won't talk, because if he did I'll tell the police about a secret that me and Eddie share.

Peter asks can I know the secret to. Crazy "K" told Eddie to tell Peter what happen to them last year. Eddie said that he wasn't going to talk about it. Crazy "K" said to Eddie can I talk about it. We are all brothers here; we should be able to say whatever. Eddie told Crazy "K" I don't care, but Peter if you here this stories you can never repeat it again. Crazy "K" started by telling Peter that him and Eddie was going to Santa Barbara for Eddie's fifteen birthdays. His mom was going to take us there. We had fun all day. His mother took us to their skate park and we had a lot of fun. Well it was late so his mother took us to a motel and there were two beds. She told me and Eddie to stay in the room. Because she was going to the store, to bring back food and something to drink, well she came back with food and beer. Eddie's mother told us that we were going to celebrate his birth. We ate and drink, Eddie and I were pretty much wasted. Well Eddie's mom told us that she was going to take a shower. I look at Eddie and told him that his mom was a hottie. Eddie told me to shut the fuck up. I told Eddie what if I took all my clothes off and took a shower with your mom what would she do. Eddie said to Crazy "K" that she would kick him out of the shower. So I said to Eddie let's see what she would do. I took all my clothes off in front of Eddie. So he would know that I was naked. I then went into the shower and his mom didn't even tell me to get out. You want to know what she said to me Peter. Peter replied yes I do what happen next. Well Crazy "K" told Peter that Eddie's mom turn around and saw that I was naked. She started to wash me and she started to go down on me. Peter asks if that meant she was sucking Crazy "K" dick. Crazy "K" said yes, and then I told her to get up and turn around. I made her turn her back towards me. I spread her legs apart and I inserted my hard cock in her wet pussy. She was enjoying it and while I was fucking her, she was saying fuck this pussy over and over. I was fucking the shit out of Eddie's mom. Crazy "K" told Peter, you know how I fuck and how I made Cindy scream. That is how I was fucking Eddie's mother. When we were done in the shower, we moved to the bed. I looked at Eddie with a big smile on my face. Eddie was looking like I kick him in the nuts. His face was all red and he was mad, but I didn't care because I was fucking a hot fucking bitch. So when we were in the bed I continued fucking her harder and harder. I give her multi-orgasms, and we fucked half the night away. After I stopped fuckin her, I told her that I needed to have a cigarette. She asks if she could have one and I give her one. I then ask if Eddie wanted one and he said no. Eddie told Crazy "K" and his mother that he didn't appreciate that they were fucking on his birthday. Eddie's mom told him that she didn't know what came over her. I told her it was because she didn't have dick in a while. I told Eddie and his mother that I wouldn't tell anybody about this, and I haven't until today.

Crazy "K" then told Peter that a couple of months went by and Eddie's mother told me that she was pregnant. She asks me if I mind if she had an abortion. I told her that I have already a child and one on the way. So I told her that she could keep it or have an abortion. It didn't matter to me, but I knew if she keep it Eddie probably would have gone insane. Eddie just looks at Crazy "K" and said fuck you man. Eddie also told Crazy "K" that the part where he gets my mother pregnant is all bull shit. Crazy "K" replied ok Eddie if you think I'll made that up fine you win. Peter, Crazy "K" told him that part I made up. Just so Eddie can sleep at night, but I'm telling the truth about that. I did get his mother pregnant that is between him and his mother.

So Crazy "K" told Peter that is why Eddie will do what I say because if he doesn't I'll tell that his mother rape me and then they will not at her. Eddie doesn't want that right Eddie. So let's keep our story straight so that the police won't be able to solve this crime. Peter replied that he wouldn't invite Crazy "K" over his house. Crazy "K" asks Peter why not. Peter replied that he wouldn't want to see him fuck his mother. Crazy "K" laughs and said I wouldn't fuck your mother because she is fat "man". Eddie and Crazy "K" started to laughs harder.

Chapter Twelve

CRAZY "K" GOES CRAZY

Well it has been a week and Peter went over to Crazy "K" pad. Peter knocks on his door and when the door opens Maria comes out. They looked at each other and they both said hi to one another. Peter asks what are you doing over here Maria replied what the fuck do you care, Peter. Maria then takes off and Peter enters the room and he sees that Sergio is putting his pants back on. Sergio tells Peter that his sister can really fuck. Peter didn't know what to make out of that. Crazy "K" comes out of the bathroom with his robe on and a cigarette hanging out of his mouth. Crazy "K" asks Peter when did you get here. Peter replied just now, Crazy "K" replied oh. Sergio told Crazy "K" that he had to go and that he really enjoy coming over to his place. Crazy "K" told Sergio no problem you are welcome to come back any time. But next time you have to bring one that we can fuck ok. Sergio said ok man next time I will. Peter looks at Crazy "K" and asks him if Sergio and he fuck his sister. Crazy "K" looks at Peter and replied of course we did. Crazy "K" also told Peter, that his sister craves cock. We just give her what she wants. Be happy that we are fucking your sister and that she isn't hoeing on the streets.

Crazy "K" asks Peter what brings you here anyway. Peter said in the newspaper, that someone found a dead body in an abandoned warehouse. Crazy "K" told Peter, so what. What does that have to do with me? So someone found a dead body in a warehouse get over it Peter. The newspaper is always reporting about people finding dead bodies. Peter stated that the paper was saying that there were three people that die almost the same way. Crazy "K" told Peter, I don't know why you are telling me this and that you better not be talking shit to Eddie either. That is all I need now is for Eddie to be all freaking out. Peter, Crazy "K" said whatever happen weeks ago get over it, you know nothing about what the paper is reporting. Crazy "K" seems upset with Peter.

Peter said oh yeah right I don't know anything that the paper was reporting. Crazy "K" told Peter to live his life and to put it out of his head. He also told Peter quit being so fucking suspicions that you know what happen to those people. Just keep your fucking mouth shut ok? Peter said that he didn't mean to make him so angry. I just wanted to tell you that it was in the paper. Crazy "K" then told Peter that he was sorry, but you can't act like you fucking know something stupid. Crazy "K" told Peter to go home and do something like get your dick suck. Peter left Crazy "K" pad and went home.

When they all meet again, it will be at school. Peter saw Eddie at the cafeteria getting something to eat. Peter goes over and he says hi to Eddie. Eddie just looks at him and tells Peter what the fuck do you want. Peter tells Eddie did you read the paper lately. Eddie told him no I haven't read the paper lately. What is in the paper? Peter told him what he read and just like Crazy "K" told Peter not to do because Eddie will freak the fuck out. Eddie drops his tray in the cafeteria. Eddie then tells Peter that they need to find Crazy "K". Eddie asks Peter do he knows where Crazy "K" is and before he could answer. Eddie told Peter to come on and that he knows where to find him. Crazy "K" was selling pot to some people in the P.E. field when they saw him.

Crazy "K" saw that they were coming his way in a hurry. Crazy "K" tells the guy what is wrong. Eddie stated that Peter told him what he read in the newspaper and that they are going to jail. Crazy "K" slaps Eddie and he falls to the ground and Crazy "K" tells Eddie to get up. Eddie gets up from the ground. He tells Eddie to control his fucking self and he looks at Peter. He grabs Peter by the throat and makes him goes to his knees. He forces his head to look at Crazy"K". He tells Peter what the fuck, I told you. You stupid fucking kid, Crazy "K" pulls out a knife and he tells Peter that he should cut his throat. Peter eyes are popping out of his head. Crazy "K" reminds Peter on what he said to him. Peter acknowledges what Crazy "K" told him. He then picks Peter up from the ground by his throat. He then throws Peter to the ground and that is when he let's go of Peter's throat. Peter was able to breathe again. While Peter was trying to get his breaths-less body going again. Crazy "K" was yelling at him see what happens when you don't listen to what I say. He turns to Eddie and kicks him in the nuts. The other people that were buying the pot ran the fuck away.

Crazy "K" put the knife away and started to hit Peter and he kicks him as well. Crazy "K" told both of them if I heard anything about what the fuck happen I'll kill both of you. They were both crying and they were scared of Crazy "K". He told both to get up and to go to their classes and act like nothing happen. He called them both fucking idiots.

When it was time for their 20 min. break Eddie and Peter saw Crazy "K" and they went the other way. Crazy "K" saw them and yelled out you guys are fucking idiots. Everybody look at Crazy "K" and he told everyone to fuck off. Peter looked back to see if Crazy "K" was following him and he saw Crazy "K" talking to the dean of boys. Peter heard Crazy "K" cuss up a storm with Mr. Roger. Mr. Roger told Crazy "K" to calm down and at that point Crazy "K" pulls out his dick and tells Mr. Roger to suck it. Everyone that saw that was laughing at Mr. Roger. Mr. Roger grabs Crazy "K" arm and takes him to his office. When Peter sees

Crazy "K" again it is lunch time and Mr. Roger is with him. Mr. Roger has Crazy "K" picking up trash.

When school is over Peter runs into Eddie. They both are talking about what happen to Crazy "K". Eddie told Peter, I told you not to mess with that guy. He is fucking crazy Peter said I know did you see what he did to Mr. Roger. Eddie said that he didn't see what happen after he left. Peter stated, that he turn around and he saw Mr. Roger talking to him and what was funny was that Crazy "K" took out his dick and told him to suck it. Eddie replied that Crazy "K" is going to get kick out of school. At that point they both run into Crazy "K". He tells both of them to get in his car. They both looked at him and Eddie said that he didn't want to because of what happen earlier. Crazy "K" said that he was sorry about that and to please get in his car. So they did get in his car and Peter asks Crazy "K" what happen with Mr. Roger. Crazy "K" told them that he has to clean the cafeteria for a while. I also have detention for about four months and I have to have a parent conference with Mr. Roger. Peter said that's it, what did Mr. Roger tell you about sucking your dick. Crazy "K" said that Mr. Roger said that I was a fuckin mental case and that he wasn't going to put up with me. He also said that I was mentally off balance. I have to see the school Psychotherapist, Peter said wow what are you going to do. Crazy"K" replied I will attend the sessions. I have to attend and that if I miss a session that I will be kicked out of the school. So I'll go and maybe I'll get a couple of kicks out of it. Eddie stated that maybe you can talk about your problem. Crazy "K" replied what is my fucking problem Eddie. Eddie said well I don't really know, but I think and don't take this the wrong way Crazy "K". But I think you are a little bit off. Crazy "K" said, to Eddie in which way. Eddie replied; well let's talk about your nickname that should say something. You like calling yourself crazy. Crazy "K" told them that he had to earn that name from his uncle. That when my uncle gave me that name, that was the proudest day of my life. Peter asks Crazy "K" whats your real name? Crazy "K" replied don't worry about that Peter you need to focuses on the situation that we are in today. My name shouldn't be the issue that we should be talking about. I should stop this car and kick your ass. But I won't just remember guys you have nothing to hide. We didn't do anything wrong. Eddie was thinking to himself that he didn't do anything wrong. That Crazy "K" was telling the truth about him. Crazy "K" told them that this Friday night we should asks some girls over my house and fuck the shit out of them. Peter agreed with Crazy "K" on that one. So Crazy "K" stops at Eddie's house to let him off. Crazy "K" told Eddie not to worry and everything will turn out fine. Crazy "K" then drove to his house and told Peter to walk the rest of the way. Peter asks Crazy "K" how come you didn't drop me off at my house. Crazy "K" replied because you acted like a bitch today. Crazy "K" also told Peter that if you ever disobey him again. Watch what will happen to you. I'll kidnap your ass and I torture you and then you will meet my purple Jesus with the big dick. Peter just looked at him and said to Crazy "K" that maybe Eddie is right that you do need some help. Crazy "K" starts to laugh and told Peter to go the fuck home and we'll talk tomorrow.

Chapter Thirteen

THE POLICE DETECTIVE ARE ASKING THE QUESTIONS

Later that night at Peter's home, him and his sister was in her room talking. They were talking about how they were missing their brother. Maria told Peter that he will be missed and that it will never be the same again. They heard a knock on the door. Peter mother came into their room and asks if they can come to the living room for a moment. When they enter the living room there were two guys sitting down on the sofa. Their mother told them that they are from the police station. One of them introduce themselves as Detective Reid and this is my partner his name is Detective Howe. Peter asks them is this about my brother's death. Det. Reid replied that we are still investigating his death still. But there have been two other killings that have similarity to your brother's death. We are here because we would like to know if you knew any of these people. Peter said, well go head I don't know if I can help you. Det. Reid asks Peter if he knew a boy name Ricky and what was his relationship to him. Peter responded yes he knew Ricky and that his brother knew him as well. So Det. Reid said was he your friend? Peter replied I knew that Robert was friends with him and I knew him from school. Det. Reid then said to Peter so he was a friend of yours. Peter said that yeah I guess he was. He was more a friend to Robert then me. Det. Reid asks Peter when the last time you saw Ricky was. Peter stated that was a while why. Det. Reid said that it wasn't important. He then asks Peter if he knew a man name Pablo. Peter replied I don't think so. Det. Howe pulls out a picture and shows Peter the picture of Pablo. Det. Reid asks Peter again if he ever saw that person. Peter told the detective no I never saw that person. Peter saw that Det. Howe was taking notes on what Peter was saying. Det. Reid asks Peter where was he the night of April 15 of this year. Peter replied oh I was staying at a friend's house. Det. Reid asks Peter which friend's house you were staying that night. Peter's mom told Det. Reid why you are asking him that. I thought that you were here to get information about Robert's death. Det. Reid told Peter's mom that they think that the deaths are relative to each other. Peter's mom asks how they are relative to each other. Det. Reid said that he wasn't allowed to answer question about an ongoing investigation. I need to know where he was staying with if he wasn't here with you. Peter's mom told Peter to tell the detective who he was with. Peter said that he was with a guy name Eddie and a guy name Crazy "K". Det. Howe was writing the names down in his little notebook. Det. Reid told Peter why you called one of your friends Crazy "K". Peter replied I do not know why, everyone just calls him that. Det. Howe shows Det. Reid something that he wrote down in his notebook. Then Det. Reid said well thanks for your cooperation in this matter. We will be in touch with any new developments with your son's case. The detectives then got up and left the house.

The next day Peter got ready for school and that he went to Crazy "K" house to tell him that the detectives were at his house last night to ask him questions about Ricky and Pablo. When Peter knocks on Crazy "K" door, he opens it and look at Peter. Peter said hey guess what happen to me last night. Crazy "K" looks at Peter and said what, did my purple Jesus with the big dick visit you last night. Peter look at him and laughed and said no cops came over and asks questions about Ricky and Pablo. Crazy "K" said Peter; let me tell you something about me, first thing in the morning. You can't come over and laugh at me when I'm talking about my purple Jesus with the big dick. I won't allow that, second who are you talking about. I don't know any guy name Pablo. Peter replied sorry about the purple thing. Crazy "K" stated oh no you didn't call my purple Jesus with the big dick. A purple thing, what if I told you and made fun of your crazy Pope dude. What do you have to say about that Peter? Peter looked puzzles and said ok that would be ok I guess. Crazy "K" told Peter quit being such a big pussy. Peter, I want you to repeat after me and say PURPLE JESUS CHRIST WITH THE BIG DICK. HELP ME AND PROTECT ME FROM ALL THE EVIL PEOPLE. Peter looked at him and before he could say anything. Crazy "K" started too yelled at him, Crazy "K" picks up his bag and told Peter I have to go to school now. They walk to his car and Crazy "K" got in and Peter thought that he would open the door so he could get in the car. But Crazy "K" back out of the driveway and left Peter just standing there. Peter said to himself that Crazy "K" is a real fuck up guy and he thinks that Mr. Roger is right by sending him to a shrink. So Peter starts to walk to school, Peter walks half way and he see Crazy "K" park at the park. Crazy "K" was sitting on his truck smoking and he yelled over to Peter to hurry up. When Peter got closes to Crazy "K" he told Peter hurry up we are going to be late. He also told Peter that the reason he made him walk was because he laughed at purple Jesus with the big dick. Nobody does that and second you keep bring up dead people to him all the time. Now when the police asks me if you Peter, had told me that they were at your house. I have to say yes and act five times crazier than normal. It's a lot of hard work and I make you guys laugh all the time. Crazy "K" told Peter to listen to what he is going to tell him. He asks Peter did you tell Eddie about the police coming to your house. Peter replied no, he then told Peter good let's keep it that way. Eddie can't deal with the pressure so let's try this again and I hope you listen. Crazy "K" told Peter in a strong voice you tell Eddie and I'll cut your fucking dick off, and you know that I can do it without even fucking blinking an eye. Peter looks at Crazy "K" and he told him that he isn't going to tell Eddie anything. Crazy "K" smiles at Peter and he say "good". Now let's go to our class before we are late. Everything was going great in school that morning. It was until the afternoon came and Mr. Roger came into Crazy "K" history class and made him go with him to his office. Crazy "K" asks Mr. Roger what did I do now. Mr. Roger stated that there are some people that want to talk with you. Crazy "K" figure that the police was there to talked to him. When they enter the office Crazy "K" was right it was the police detectives. They told Crazy "K" to have a seat because they wanted to ask him some questions.

In this part of the story that you will read I will have to reveal Crazy "K" real name. Because the police doesn't called him by his nickname "crazy" but they use his real name. But I can not reveal his true identity in this book, so in this portion of the story the detectives will call him "K". I will reveal his true identity in another book.

Det. Reid tells "K" what has happen in the past weeks and can he help them and try to solve some of the mystery. "K" looks at Det. Reid and tells him that he would try, but he knows nothing about any murders. Det. Reid asks "K" where you were on the night of April 15 of this year. "K" told him that on that night he was at home. Det. Reid asks if he was alone that night. "K" said no, I think I had friends over. Det. Reid then states to "K" who was over and can you please give me their names. "K" looks at the detective and he said no, I don't remember who it was. Det. Reid asks how come, "K" told him I have a real hard time of retaining things in my head. Det. Howe said do you know a kid name Peter. "K" replied yes I do know that guy. He then asks "K" was he at your place that night. "K" responded by saying I don't remember who was at my place that night. It was a long time, you guys should of asks me that then. Det. Reid asks well what do you remember about that night. "K" thinks for a while and said I think I was smoking some pot and jacking off in the shower. I like doing that in the shower. Do you guys like jacking off in the shower? Det. Reid tells "K" to take this seriously. "K" looks at him and said that he is taking this seriously. Det. Reid told "K" to leave the bull shit on the playground and not here when they are asking question about people being murdered. "K" told Det. Reid that he knows nothing about people being murder. Det. Reid tells "K" do you know these guys and he shows a picture of Robert and Ricky. "K" said yes I know those guys. Did you know that they were killed? "K" said yes I know that they were killed, they were my friends. Det. Reid said what were your relationship to these guys, "K" responded by saying if you think that I was fucking them I wasn't. Det. Reid said why would you say that? Well "K" told them that Robert and Ricky were fucking fagots. Det. Reid asks how I knew that. "K" told the detectives that he was fucking a girl and Robert was there watching him and when he was done. Robert wanted me to fuck him and I told Robert I don't swing like that. But if you like dick I know people that are gay. I introduce Robert to Red's gang and Ricky was in it. Det. Reid asks "K" if he knew that Juan (aka Red) rape Robert in the boys shower at school. "K" told them that he was there when Juan was fucking Robert in the shower. Det. Reid told "K" why didn't you come forward and reported this. "K" told them that it wasn't he's business to do that, if Robert wanted to stay in the closest it wasn't going to be me to bring him out. Remember I like these guys and I didn't have a problem with them being gay. Det. Reid asks "K" so then you know Robert's brother Peter. "K" said yes I do? Det. Reid said was Peter there the night of April 15. I guess he might have been I have a lot of people over. Well then did Peter ever tell you that he wanted to catch his brother killers, said Det. Reid. "K" told the detectives will no, but he wasn't for sure about you guys catching anyone. "K" then ask the detectives should I have my mother here while answering these questions. They look at each other and stated to him, why should you have your mother here. "K" said to them because I'm a minor and that you might want to suck my dick or something. "K" also told them that he doesn't have to answer any more questions. Det. Reid was getting angry and told "K" that I can take you to the station, son if you don't be cooperative. "K" told Det. Reid don't call me son again ok? Det. Reid said what did you say. "K" responded you are not my daddy if you were my daddy, I would jump up and if my mama' was here I would slap her across the face. For fucking such an asshole of a man that you are. You think because you have a badge you can tell people what the fuck to do. Fuck you ass hole. Det. Reid told "K" you can go to the station and wait for your mother? That you don't have to play the crazy part with me. "K" told them that he didn't have to hear this shit and that he was going back to class. When "K" turns his back and was going to walk out. Det. Reid grabs "K" and throws him on the ground and handcuffs "K". He tells him that he is going to the police station. "K" starts to yell and starts to cuss at them. The detectives had to carry him out of school. "K" was trying to kick them so the detectives hog tied the boy. Then Det. Reid grabs "K" by the hair. "K" tries not to look at him. So he pulls "K" hair until his head is facing the detective. Det. Reid asks "K" to stop acting like a fucking animal and that they were going to take him to the station for more questioning. "K" told them to fuck off PIGS? Det. Reid picks up "K" by hair and "K" told them that he is going to sue the fucking city. Because "K" thought that this kind of treatment from the police was police brutality. Crazy "K"'s mom pick him up from the police station. Later that night Crazy "K" called Peter tells him that they will have to walk to school on the next day.

Chapter Fourteen

HARASSMENT FROM THE POLICE

The next day Crazy "K" was walking to school with Peter and Eddie. When they were walking, Crazy "K" told them that he should have gotten his car last night. Eddie wasn't very talkative when they were heading to school. Crazy "K" told Eddie that he needed his cock suck and that will put a smile on his face. Crazy "K" said that Rachel was going to be at the football field and that she will gave him the best blowjob before school. He also said that because Rachel sucks his dick he received a 100% on a test. Peter told Crazy "K" that Rachel was a nice girl and that he is interested in her. Crazy "K" told Peter, you can't fall in love with a whore. Peter replied that she isn't a whore. Crazy "K" told Peter, just because she fucked you that doesn't mean to make her your girl. Anyway she likes to suck a lot of cock. Crazy "K" stated that if we hurry up maybe there will be an enough time before school starts that she can suck all three of our dicks.

At that point a car pulls up and they notice that it was the detectives. They wanted to ask some more questions. Det. Reid asks the boys if they were going to school. Crazy "K" told them that they were headed in that direction. The car stop and Det. Reid got out of the car. Det. Reid asks Peter that he heard that he wanted to kill the person that killed his brother. Det. Reid also said that Pablo was on their list of prime suspect. Crazy "K" said to the police, well then you did your job. Det. Reid told the boys that their job has changed now that Pablo was killed. Crazy "K" told the guys that we don't know the guy. Det. Reid stated that we know Peter was very upset about losing your brother. He also told Peter that his brother knew Pablo and that Pablo's brother Juan was in jail because of what happen in the shower. Det. Reid said that since Robert and Juan were having a relationship maybe you though that Pablo killed your brother. Crazy "K" told his friends that they are going to be late. Det. Reid told the boys why are you guys in such a hurry. Crazy "K" told the Det. Reid that they were going to get their cocks suck before school. Det. Reid told Crazy "K" to shut up and to go if he wanted to. Because they want to talk to Peter and that they know Peter knows something about the three murders. Crazy "K" told the detectives to go fuck themselves. He also told Peter that they are just rattling your emotions and that they are stupid cops. Crazy "K" told the detectives that if they think that Peter is a killer. Then I'm the fucking President.

So they started to walk off and Det. Reid told them that he will be keeping an eye on them. Eddie is freaking out and Peter is worry as well. Crazy "K" told them to come on Rachel won't be there much longer. When they reach the football field they see Rachel. Crazy "K" tells her let's go to the other side of the field. Crazy "K" tells Rachel to suck his dick and then she can do the other guys. Crazy "K" unzipped his pants and pulled out his dick. Rachel took a hold of it and she started to suck his dick. Eddie told Crazy "K" that he thought that he was going to be first. Crazy "K" told Eddie that he will be next. Rachel was giving a blow job to Crazy "K". Eddie and Peter were talking about what just happen a little while ago. They were started to get on Crazy "K" nerves. Crazy "K" pushes Rachel away from is cock. He tells the guys to shut the fuck up. Don't you see that I'm trying to enjoy this blowjob? Crazy "K" puts back his semi-hard cock back in his pants. He then tells Rachel to give Eddie a blow job. Crazy "K" said to Eddie go ahead man get your dick suck. Eddie goes over to Rachel and she pulls out his dick. Rachel starts to give him a blowjob. When Crazy "K" seeing that Eddie is enjoying it. Crazy "K" starts to talk to Peter. He tells Peter did you see that cop look at us. I think he knows what happen that night. Eddie is listening to Crazy "K" and now Eddie can't concentrate on Rachel giving him a blow job. When Crazy "K" sees that he is fucking up Eddie blow job. He tells Eddie do you like being distracted from Rachel sucking your dick. You don't like it very much. That is what happens when you and Peter were talking and Rachel was sucking my cock. Rachel gets up and she said that she isn't going to suck anyone's dick. Rachel then walks away; Eddie had his dick hanging out of his pants. Crazy "K" tells Eddie to put his dick back in his pants. Eddie seems upset and Crazy "K" told Eddie we are even and the next time I'm getting a blowjob you and pussy boy will shut the fuck up.

After school everyone meets at Crazy "K" car. Peter tells them that the detectives are waiting at the entrance of the parking lot. Crazy "K" told Peter that they don't know anything about Ricky and Pablo. They are just trying to make you nervous so they can think there on the right track. Eddie said that they what to talk to him about Peter. Crazy "K" asks Eddie when they told you this. Eddie replied today, he was call out of his class and he had to report to Mr. Roger's office. Peter asks Eddie what did they asks you. Eddie replied they wanted me to tell them if you wanted revenge on the people that killed your brother. I told them that I knew nothing and that you didn't tell me anything. I also told them that we weren't that close and the only thing we had in commend was that we knew Crazy "K". Peter said well, I guess that makes you get off the hook. I guess that make the police looks at me like I did everything by myself. Crazy "K" told Peter; if you get caught don't bring us down with you. Peter replied what the fuck I'm support to take the rap for everything. Crazy "K" told Peter yes you do because he was your brother and not ours. Peter starts to cry and Crazy "K" told Peter to stop that and that the detectives are watching us. Let's get out of here and talk at my place about this.

They all got in Crazy "K"'s car and left the school. When Crazy "K" was driving, he notices the police was following him. When he told the guys this, Eddie started to freak out. Crazy "K" told Eddie to calm the fuck down and that this is a police tacted. Eddie asks how he knew that. Crazy "K" replied that his uncle told him that the police do things like this to rattle you. The cops think that we know something about the murders so they are going to bug us until one of us breaks down. Crazy "K" tells them which one will it be, who will be the first one to go to them. Peter said it won't be me. Eddie also said that it won't be him either. Crazy "K" told Eddie that they were going to stay at his house for awhile. Eddie told them whatever. When they got to Eddie's house and Crazy "K" parks his car, the police just drove by.

Once they enter Eddie's house they all saw Eddie's mom wasted on liquor and drugs. Eddie told his mother to go and lay down. Eddie's mom told Crazy "K" did he want to fuck her pussy. Before Crazy "K" could say anything Eddie told his mother that Peter was there to. Peter said hi my name is Peter. Eddie's mom replied so what, do you want to lick my pussy boy. That made her laugh and she told them that Eddie gets upset with her talking like that. Eddie replied to his mother and said yes I do mom. Especially when you are trying to fuck my friends and that is why I don't invite people over. Eddie's mom said to Crazy "K" come on let's go to my room and she takes Crazy "K"'s hand. Peter tells Eddie what you are going to do about them. Eddie replies nothing I do will stop my mom from fucking him. Peter sees all the drugs on the table and asks Eddie why does she needs all of these drugs. Eddie told Peter that he better not tell anyone about what he sees at his house. Peter replies that he wouldn't. They hear

Crazy "K" and Eddie's mom fucking in her bedroom. Eddie turns on the T.V. to drown out his mother morns and her screaming. But Peter stills hear the noises that are coming out of the room. Peter is thinking man Crazy "K" must be fucking the shit out of her. An hour and a half goes by Crazy "K" walks in to the room with his clothes in his arms. Crazy "K" asks Peter if he wants to fuck Eddie's mom to. Eddie stated that Peter is not going to fuck his mother to that is all I need.

Crazy "K" told Peter to fuck her and that she is waiting for him. Crazy "K" told Peter that he wants to talk to Eddie by himself. Eddie then replied to Crazy "K" that Peter should go home if he needed to talk to him alone and that Peter didn't need to her. Crazy "K" told Peter to go in there and fuck her. Peter said that if Eddie didn't want him to do that why should he. Crazy "K" replied because I told you to and that she wants to, that is why. Peter gets up and walks towards her bedroom. When Peter enters her room, he saw Eddie's mom naked and she told him to take off his clothes. Peter said are you sure you want me to fuck you. She replied yes I do want you to fuck me. That made Peter get an instant boner. She told Peter to come closer and she started to take off his pants. When that happen she saw that Peter had a boner and she started to suck his dick. Peter was so excited that he began to fuck her mouth. He was putting his dick in her mouth after fifteen minutes he nutted in her mouth. Peter said sorry for nutting in her mouth. She sallow it and told Peter don't worry about it. She then told Peter that she needed to go and sleep for awhile. Peter got up and put his clothes back on before he went back to the guys. When Peter went back to the living room he saw Crazy "K" forcing pills down Eddie's throat. Peter asks Crazy "K" what the fuck are you doing to Eddie. Crazy "K" told Peter that Eddie needs to try and commits suicide. Peter said why, Crazy "K" told Peter, Eddie needs to be hospitalize so when he tells the police on what happens they won't believe him, because he tried to commits suicide. Peter couldn't believe what Crazy "K" was doing, he told Crazy "K" to stop. Crazy "K" told Peter to call

911, but don't say anything just leave the phone off the hook. They send a police car to check it out. Crazy "K" told Peter just do it. Peter picks up the phone and he dials 911 and he drops the phone. Crazy "K" told Peter let's get the fuck out of here. Crazy "K" takes a look outside before they leave the house. He doesn't see anyone around and then they left. Crazy "K" tells Peter that he had to make Eddie look like he is crazy. Because I think he is going to turn us in to the police. Eddie knows too much and if we don't do something about it he'll open his mouth. Peter said I think Eddie wouldn't turn us in man. Crazy "K" replied back will see about that. Peter said what if the police are to later and he dies. Crazy "K" said if he dies then we have nothing to worry about. But if he doesn't we can say he is a crack head. Peter looks at Crazy "K" and tells him you are crazy. Crazy "K" replied to Peter and said thanks man.

But the police did come in time and they arrested Eddie's mom. Because Eddie overdose on her drugs and Eddie was admit to the hospital for drug treatment.

Chapter Fifteen

SUICIDE

Well it was all over the neighborhood that Eddie tried to commit suicide and that his mom was in jail. Crazy "K" and Peter visited Eddie in the hospital. They went to the front desk to see what room number he was. Peter asks the receptionist if she knew Eddie and what room was he in. She replied that he was in the mental ward. That is on the first floor and you enter at your own risk. She also stated that we couldn't bring any gifts to him at this time. So they went into the ward for crazy people. Peter wanted to be funny and he told Crazy "K" that he should feel right at home. Crazy "K" just looked at Peter and smile thanks fucker.

When they enter the room and Crazy "K" saw who else was there he said fuck. Peter look and that saw that it was the detectives. Det. Reid said hi boys we were just about done here. Det. Reid got up and told Peter to seat in his seat and Peter replied no thanks I'll stand. Det. Reid told Eddie that if he needed to talk some more just call him and he will come back. The detective left the room. Eddie told them that the detectives were asking question about my attempt to commit suicide. Crazy "K" told Eddie so what did you tell them. Eddie told them that he didn't feel like talking about it. Crazy "K" told Eddie, you'll right just take it easy Eddie. We just want you to get better and please don't try that again.

Crazy"K" told Eddie, I know you have a lot on your mind. You know on what happen before you try to commit suicide. On how you were telling me that you didn't want to live anymore because your mother was a fucking whore. Did you tell the detectives that we were fucking your mother? Eddie replied that he didn't say anything to the detectives. Crazy "K" told Eddie to put that incident out of your head. All we want you to do now is to get better Eddie. We'll leave you alone so you can rest. So they both left Eddie there and told him that they will return later.

When they were going through the lobby, Det. Reid stops them. He asks the boys why Eddie would try to kill himself. Crazy "K" replied how we would know that. Det. Reid said well maybe something was bugging him. Crazy "K" said hey something was bugging Eddie. Det. Reid asks what that was. Crazy "K" told Det. Reid that Eddie wouldn't want him to speak about what he told me. Det. Reid then says well maybe if you told us we could help your friend out. Crazy "K" told the detectives that I respect my friends to much too ever tell someone else what we were talking about. Det. Reid told that Eddie will be in here for a while guys. Maybe you can help him by giving the doctors here a heads up on his condition. Crazy "K" said ok, tell the doctors to ask him about his mother sex life. Det. Reid replied what that has to do with him. Crazy "K" said you ask for a heads up on his condition. I just give you one; Crazy "K" told Peter, let's get the fuck out of here. Det. Reid said to Peter that one day we will know the truth about certain things. Peter replied what does that mean. Det. Reid said I know that you guys are involved in Ricky and Pablo murders. We just don't have an enough evident to charge you with their murders. Peter was surprise by what Det. Reid told them. Crazy "K" told the detective to fuck off man. Peter said to Det. Reid that he didn't murder anyone and if they work as hard as trying to pin two people's murders on him. That they would have found the true murders and they would have found his brother's killers to. Det. Reid told Peter that the tracks lead to you guys. Peter told them that they are very wrong in thinking that we are the ones. Crazy "K" told Peter, to come on and let's get out of here.

Crazy "K" and Peter got in the car and they left the hospital. Peter said can you believe these cops. Crazy "K" said to Peter, well at lease they are just looking at you right now. As Crazy "K" was driving he pulls out a cigarette and started to smoke. Peter asks Crazy "K" why he said they are just looking at me. Crazy "K" told Peter that he told him that the police was going to do that. Because of your brother's death, they know that people goes a little crazy when their love ones are killed. Crazy "K" told Peter let's go and get some pussy. Peter said ok, that's sound real good to me. Peter asks Crazy "K" where is the pussy at. Crazy "K" replies, well we can't get any pussy from Eddie's mom and they both laugh.

Crazy "K" said to Peter that we can go to Carlos to see what he is doing. Peter replied that he knew the guy. Crazy "K" told Peter that his sister likes to give head. When they got to Carlos home Crazy "K" knocks on the door. An old lady answers the door and when she saw that Crazy "K" was there she started to yell at him. Peter then saw that a Carlos came out of the house. Crazy "K" asks Carlos if he wanted to get high. Carlos replied yes, do you have some pot on you. Crazy "K" told Peter to go in the car and open the glove compartment. Peter went to the car and opens the compartment and took out a big bag of weed. He took out the bag and return to Crazy "K". Carlos said that is a big bag, Crazy "K" told Carlos let's go to your tree house. Peter look at them and said aren't you a little big for a tree house. Carlos says maybe but it is the only place I can keep my pipes and weed. Without my mom throwing away my shit, he then told them to go around the house to the backyard. When they reach the backyard Carlos was coming out of the house. His mother came out as well. She told Crazy "K" that she didn't like him being at her house. Carlos told his mother to go back inside and that Crazy "K" was going to behaves himself. Carlos told Crazy "K", to tell his mother that you will be nice. Crazy "K" told Carlos's mother that he will behave and that she didn't need to worry. Carlos's mother went back into the house, and they went up the tree to smoke their pot.

They all were getting high and Crazy "K" asks Carlos if his sister was home. Carlos said that she was, but she was not going to come over here to fuck you. Crazy "K" told Carlos that he will give him forty dollars if you bring your sister over here. Carlos replied to him by saying that she is not going to come over here to fuck you. Crazy "K" told Carlos whatever happens I'll still give you forty dollars. Carlos said I'll try Carlos then took a little rock and he throws it at his sister's window. She looked out the window and Carlos told her that Crazy "K" was here. She came outside and up the tree and she said to Crazy "K" hi. Crazy "K" replied hi, there Sally. She said who is your friend; Crazy "K" said that his name is Peter. Sally said what do you guys what to do. Crazy "K" said to Sally, do we have to say it, I think you know what I want. Sally laughs and she takes his joint and starts to smoke it. Sally was starting to get high and then she crawls to Crazy "K". Sally started to take off his pants and she pulled off his boxer. Everyone saw that Crazy "K" had a boner. Sally started to suck his dick and that Crazy "K" was likely it. It took 20 minutes for Crazy "K" to blow his load. Sally took a drink of soda to wash the cum down her throat. Sally turns around and asks Peter if he wanted a blow job? Peter told Sally ok, Sally told Peter to take off his pants. Sally also asks Crazy "K" to fuck her from behind. So Sally took off her dress and bent down to suck Peter's cock. She then cocks up her ass so that Crazy "K" could insert his fat dick in her wet pussy. Sally was sucking Peter's dick and Crazy "K" was pounding his cock in her pussy. When it was over Carlos ask for the forty dollars and Crazy "K" give him the money.

Crazy "K" and Peter got back into the car and Crazy "K" took Peter back to his house. When they got there, they saw the detective car's park down the street. Peter look at Crazy "K" and told him that he was getting tired of them bugging him. Crazy

"K" told Peter to not let them get to you. You have to stay strong and not let them see that they are getting to you Peter. Crazy "K" told Peter to get some rest and that he'll pick up him tomorrow.

Chapter Sixteen

COVERING UP A MURDER TO LOOK LIKE A SUICIDE

When Crazy "K" picks up Peter the next day he told Peter that they weren't going to school today. Peter asks Crazy "K" what we are going to do. Crazy "K" told him that we can go and hang out at the park for a while. Crazy "K" told Peter that he had a bottle of whiskey and that he thought that Peter needed a drink. When they got to the park he parks his car. They both got out of the car. Crazy "K" pulls out a pack of cigarettes and asks Peter if he wanted one. Peter took one and Crazy "K" lit Peter's cigarette. Crazy "K" then took out the bottle of whiskey and told Peter to drink some. Peter took the bottle and he started to drink it. Crazy "K" told Peter that he didn't feel comfortable with him and that he thought that Peter will crack under the pressure that the police was bearing on him. Peter told Crazy "K" that he could with stand the pressure and that he wouldn't talk. Crazy "K" told Peter that he type up a suicide note for him. Peter was shock that Crazy "K" was telling him this.

Crazy "K" gave Peter the note and he read it out loud. After Peter read the note, he look at Crazy "K" and said that he wasn't going to do it. Crazy "K" gave Peter the bottle of whiskey again and told him to drink the bottle. Peter wanted to say no, but Crazy "K" took out a 38 revolver. Crazy "K" told Peter that he would shoot him in the head if he didn't drink the whiskey. Peter did what he was asking to do and he drinks the whole bottle of whiskey. Crazy "K" told Peter that his family should be all out of the house. Peter stated that he didn't what to die and that he didn't want his family to find him. Crazy "K" put his arm around him and told Peter that he will call 911 when he starts. Peter was still in shock and Crazy "K" helps Peter back into the car. Crazy "K" took Peter back to his house. Crazy "K" told Peter to give his house key to him. Peter did and Crazy "K" helps Peter to his bedroom. Crazy "K" told Peter that he'll return in a little bit. Crazy "K" left Peter's house and he drove his car two blocks away. He then walks back to Peter's house. It was around 11:15am when Crazy "K" got back to Peter's house. He keeps the house key that Peter gave him. When Crazy "K" enters Peter's room he saw that Peter was a sleep. Crazy "K" then went into the bathroom and started to fill the bathtub up with hot water. Once the bathtub was filling up half way, he then went back to Peter's room. He helps Peter to get undress and Peter asks if it was time to die. Crazy "K" told Peter that he wasn't going to kill him. It was only to let the police know that Peter wanted to be left alone. Crazy "K" put Peter in the tub and Crazy "K" took out a new razor. But before Crazy "K" was going to help Peter kill himself, he played the song that was title someone save my life tonight. While the song was playing Crazy "K" picks up Peter's left wrist and he takes the razor blade and opens up his vein. Peter started to cry and Crazy "K" told him again that he will call for help before he dies. Crazy "K" takes the other wrist and opens the vein on that arm. Peter is bleeding in the bathtub, Peter asks for help. Crazy "K" told Peter that he isn't going to call anyone and that he had to die. Peter started to cry and he tries to put up a fight. But Peter could not because he of was drunk and he was losing a lot blood. Peter finally passes out and Crazy "K" knew that Peter would be able to get out and call for help. Crazy "K" turns around and locks the door of the bathroom. Crazy "K" opens the window and climb out of the window. Crazy "K" left Peter's backyard and he began to walks towards his car. When he reaches his car he gets in and drives to his uncle's friend's house for an alibi. Crazy "K" told his uncle's friend Frank want had happen in the past months. Frank was upset but he told Crazy "K" that he would be his alibi. Frank told Crazy "K" to drive by Peter's house and if he saw the police there stop and asks what had happen. Remember that you came to me at 9:00am to talk about your friend was thinking about committed suicide. It was about 4:45pm and that Crazy "K" started to drive by Peter's house. He saw that there were all of the emergency vehicles and the police cars at Peter's house. Crazy "K" stops and parks his car and went up where a crowd was forming.

Crazy "K" asks what happen and someone said that the boy that lived there kill himself. At that moment Det. Reid saw Crazy "K" in the crowd and he pulls him out and he asks Crazy "K" what happen here. Crazy "K" told Det. Reid that he didn't know Peter was serious about killing himself. Det. Reid told Crazy "K" what made him do it. Crazy "K" was starting to cry and he started to yell at Det. Reid and told him that it was their fault that Peter is dead. Det. Reid said what did you said. Crazy "K" replied that you pressure the kid and he couldn't take it and that is why Peter is dead. Det. Reid told Crazy "K" where you were today. Crazy "K" told Det. Reid that he was with an old friend and his name was frank.

Det. Reid told Crazy "K" that he knows all about his past and that he thinks that Crazy "K" knew something about Peter killing himself. Crazy "K" was throwing a fit and cussing up a storm. Crazy "K" said that the police made my friend kill himself. Det. Reid said to Crazy "K" to go home and that they will talk later. Crazy "K" got in his car and he made up a song for Peter.

He began to sing that song and the words are "they called him Peter".

Crazy "K" made it home and he was taking a shower, when he heard someone banging on his door. Crazy "K" got out of the shower and he put a towel around him so he could answers the door. When he opens the door it was Maria and she was very upset. Maria asks Crazy "K" why her brother Peter took his own life. Crazy "K" told Maria to come inside and that they could talk. Crazy "K" offer Maria a cigarette but she refuses it. So Crazy "K" lit his cigarette and told Maria that the detective was bugging Peter. About Ricky and this guy name Pablo murders. I guess that the police thought that Peter had something do with it. Maria was crying when she mention that Peter left a suicide note. Crazy "K" asks Maria what was in the note. Maria told him that Peter confess in the note that he killed Ricky by cutting off his penis and throat. Peter then stated that he killed Pablo for revenge. Maria also said that Peter asks forgiveness from his parents and that he couldn't go to jail. So he decides to take his life, because the police was going to find out about the murders that he committed.

Crazy "K" knows that the police will soon leave him alone. Crazy "K" took off his towel and he told Maria that he was going to fuck her. He also told Maria that fucking her will take her mind off Peter's death. Maria started to take her clothes off and she lay on the bed and told Crazy "K" to start fucking her. Crazy "K" pulls on Maria's legs to spread them apart. He sucks his finger and he put it in her pussy. He was rubbing her pussy and was getting her pussy all wet. Once her pussy was real wet he inserted his dick in her pussy. Crazy "K" began to fuck her and he was sucking her tits. He was fucking Maria real hard she was making all different kinds of noises and that made Crazy "K" to fuck her even harder. He fuck her at least an hour, I guess Maria told her parents that she want to come over Crazy "K"'s house to find out about Peter. When Crazy "K" was finish fucking her, he got up and put his robe on and he then open his door. Maria father was outside and he told Crazy "K" that he heard him fucking his daughter. Able yelled into the house, he told Maria you fucking whore get dress and come out of his house. Crazy "K" told Able to calm down that Maria needed to have his cock in her. Able slapped Crazy "K" and told him to never come to his house again. When Maria left the house Able slapped her and grab her by the arm. When they left Crazy "K" thought that her father was wrong for going off like that.

The next day Crazy "K" visited Eddie in the hospital, he told Eddie what happen to Peter. Eddie flapped the fuck out and started to scream and throw thing around. The orderly and the nurses had to restrain him and they drag him out of the visiting room. The nurse came and asks him what did you tell Eddie. Crazy "K" replied that he just told him that his friend Peter committed suicide. The nurse told him to leave and if he came back you don't tell a person that tried to kill himself. That a friend succeeds in doing what he wanted to do. Crazy "K" said that he didn't think of that, he just wanted Eddie to know. Crazy "K" left and he was smiling that he didn't get caught in all this crap.

THE END